ISTORIA BOOKS
presents

Mending Ruth's Heart

A novel by Libby Sternberg

Cover by Amanda Kelsey, Razzle Dazzle design

Get on the Istoria Books mailing list!
Subscribers learn of special limited-time-only discounts. Sign up at the website where you can also view other Istoria Books titles:
www.IstoriaBooks.com

Copyright 2012 Libby Sternberg

ISBN-13: 978-0615674889
ISBN-10: 0615674887

Books written by Libby Sternberg are available through the author's official website:
www.LibbySternberg.com

Other Istoria Books titles are available through the publisher's website where you can sign up to receive news of the sequel to this book:
www.IstoriaBooks.com

To my daughter, Hannah,
a wonderful writer in her own right

Prologue

March 1904

MY MOTHER THINKS my heart has hardened. Every day she looks to soften it, but I must admit her efforts only seem to thicken the callous that grows on that unseen organ. Or at least it feels so to me, with her regular urging to "get out and visit friends" or "take a ride to Grandma's" or "come with me to church this Sunday, won't you, dear?" or, worst of all—"black makes you look jaundiced, you could at least try on that deep blue suit I had made for you. You are still young, Ruth, just over nineteen...."

With every admonition, I feel myself recoiling ever further from the gentle rubbing against humanity that would, perhaps, tenderize my outlook. Was it ever so with mothers and daughters—why do we pull away from the one who cherished and led us before we knew the world?

I have been this way for six months now, ever since my fiancé, Miguel deTorquescero, was lost in a mud slide on the Big Sur, that cruel landscape that dares the Pacific to take it down. Well, the sea conspired with the skies that day, unleashing storms that blended both waters into a massive flood, the two claiming victory over the proud earth, bringing it low, teaching it not to be so boastful.

My beloved, returning to Carmel Valley with six fine ponies for the new small ranch at which I was to be matriarch—assuming God blessed us with children some day—was lost along with the horses. It was by the grace of God, or so says Mother, that Father wasn't lost, as well. He'd witnessed the whole catastrophe.

Shaken by the incident, Mother stayed very close to Father the week after it happened, often talking to him in his language—Spanish—instead of the English that she'd spoken since childhood. Her grammar was good if her accent poor. When she said "*corazon*," she never enunciated the wispy "z" correctly, pronouncing it with the precision of Mr. Leiden, our Teutonic grocer in town, instead of the fluidity of a Spaniard.

For a week after the tragic event, I was stricken mute and ill, unable even to go to the memorial service, which, since his body had not been found, seemed a betrayal to me. How could they be so sure that Miguel had perished? Perhaps a thump to the head had dazed him and he wandered, lost in direction and mind, searching for a love he felt but could not name.

That comforted me for some time after. That is, until the remains washed on the rocks. A proper burial took place then. And I managed to stay upright at least, if not sociable. But, oh, what a struggle it was to hear the useless words of comfort, especially from the priest. I know the poor fellow was well-meaning, but how could a merciful God take Miguel away from me? Was I so small in His eyes that He deemed I did not deserve love? I ponder this daily.

Never an over-talkative woman, I became even more miserly with my speech after that, finding consoling communion with other mute animate beings—the yarrow that sparkles in the sun on the byways of the valley, the towering redwoods that pierce the sky, the gentle mewing lambs and bellowing cows on my parents' wide spread.

My father seems to understand. He says little to me while I help him work the ranch, just a nod here or a hat tip there, sometimes a tiny smile that only I can read.

I am my father's daughter, with raven hair and honey skin, the blood of the conquistadors running through my veins. My younger brother, Josephus, stole some of my mother's fairer traits. His hair, while curly, glints gold on clear days, and his skin, while not pale, looks sun-touched rather than blood-warmed. He is a rascal, prone to teasing, a year younger than I.

He fits in, while I always feel a bit apart, not quite belonging to either the world of my mother or my father. Miguel had grounded me. Now I am adrift again.

Chapter One

Two years later

DUSTY AND HOT, I approached the ranch house. Before I pulled off my gloves, I knew something was different. I'd already noticed my grandparents' buckboard horses feeding in the corral closest to the barn. I'd seen their rig nearby. They didn't get out much these days—we go to them to visit—so my surprise turned to dread as my feet clomped up the two steps to the wide porch.

Before entering, I overheard something that made me pause. My mother's voice, clear and direct.

"It's not right to grieve so long. The Bible says—"

"That argument is hardly likely to persuade her," my father said, his warm accent a mere whisper in his perfect English. "She feels abandoned by her faith."

"It's not healthy, though," my mother remonstrated. "She's gotten thinner. Her hair is limp and dull. She wears nothing but black…."

"Throw away those clothes as soon as they wear out," my practical grandfather, Daniel Winchester, remarked. "Buy her new in every color under the sun."

At that, my grandmother, Kit, chuckled softly. "Unfortunately, Sarah is such a clever seamstress that Ruth's clothes are likely to last a dozen years before she'll need more."

"Thank you for the compliment," Mother replied. "But you see what I'm up against. She could go on like this for years."

"She needs a mission, something to do," Grandmother Kit went on. "She needs something to help her get past this. It has become the center of her world."

"She needs a change," my father interjected. "On that we can agree."

"She needs a new love," my mother murmured, "but that is out of our hands."

My face flamed. Of course my mother would seek to replace Miguel in my heart. She never had been fond of him, once even suggesting to me that he needed to be more careful with his money. But he'd used it to buy a spread for us, for me, so that we'd not be dependent on either of our families. He'd borrowed, yes, to stake the claim, but it had been a good investment—had he lived. As it was, it had been sold off at his death, and the money given to his sister, Anita, and her young husband, a bequest of which I'd approved.

I was about to storm away, but a hand on my shoulder startled me. Turning, I saw my smiling brother, a finger to his lips, urging me to shush. Now a conspirator with him, my mood relaxed, and we both continued to eavesdrop.

"Maybe they'll say something about me," Joe whispered.

But they didn't—they kept talking about me, and it was a wonder to behold how they had mapped out my future without my consent. It seemed this meeting had been convened so that I would go back to Grandmother and Grandfather's house with them—they'd contrived a suitable excuse for this necessity.

Being of advanced years, my grandparents needed "someone to help oversee" the running of their household since their housekeeper, Maria, had just left to be married. I guessed that my parents knew I'd see through this ruse without the presence of my grandparents to persuade me. Saying no to them would be far more difficult than putting off my mother had she suggested this scheme alone.

Squaring my shoulders, I prepared for battle, however. I would not let sentiment—or my great affection for my grandparents—rule. After they'd worked out the last detail of this magnificent plan, I entered the parlor, letting the door slam behind me, which caused Joe to shout in protest.

"I'm not going anywhere," I said with conviction. I bent to kiss my grandmother and did the same for Grandfather Daniel. "I can recommend new help for you, if you'd like. But I am quite content here. Now, if you'll excuse me, I have some chores to finish."

I was about to head toward the back of the house and out to my unnamed tasks when my father's voice stopped me, strong and commanding.

"Ruth Consuela Sanchez, you will come back here and show proper respect. Your grandparents traveled to visit with you, and you can at least spare a few moments to show your appreciation. It troubles me that you would not see that retreating to engage in make-work is both insult and offense. That is not the girl I raised."

A man of few words, he stopped me with this heart-slapping speech. I turned, but my expression remained grave.

"I'm sorry, Father…and Grandmother and Grandfather," I said, nodding toward them. "But I could not help but overhear you contriving to think of things for me to do. Surely it is not unreasonable for me to be troubled by such talk and want to smooth my temper before it makes for worse offense than my absence."

At this, Father did not balk. "Then, control your temper. You let it rule you too often. You will stay here and be amiable."

No one else spoke, so his command seemed to have created the exact opposite effect, igniting nervous tension instead of calm. I had to inwardly smile. My father was a strong presence. He had overcome the objections of my grandparents when courting my mother, I was told, by making it clear that, while he wished for their blessing and would work hard to earn it, he'd not tolerate any misperceptions about his heritage. Mother often said I'd inherited my "stubbornness" from him.

"As for our plans, I have but one for you." Now he looked around at the rest of the assembled, even Joe, who'd managed to grab a lemon cookie from a tray near the chair where Grandmother sat.

"Papa, I know you want what's best for me—"

"No. I do not. Or at least, I do not know what is best for you any longer, my *niña*" he said with grim determination. "I do know, however, what is best for me and your mother. We need an agent to negotiate with the Southern Pacific managers in San Francisco who we believe are overcharging us for our feed shipments here and our beef shipments north. I was going to go, but I don't want to leave the ranch during foaling season. You will go in my stead."

My mouth dropped open. Mother's eyes widened. My grandmother and grandfather smiled. Joe frowned and nearly spat out his cookie.

"I could do that, Father!" he said.

"Yes, he could," I said in one of the few moments of agreement with my brother. "Better than I. And it is not yet foaling season." I crossed my arms over my chest, glaring at him.

"No!" my father bellowed. "Josephus's strong hands are needed here. And you, Ruth, are quite capable of arguing with any man. You have a quick tongue when you choose to use it. If you can not let go of the wrath that colors your disposition, then at least use it in the family's service by flinging it upon the agents of the Southern Pacific. I will accept no argument."

My mother, who'd watched this interaction with wide eyes, chimed in. "And it *will* be foaling season by the time we've outfitted you for the trip," she said.

And that was how I ended up, in the year 1906, planning to go to San Francisco, my black wardrobe thrown away, and my grief ripped from my heart as if a scab had been pulled from a festering wound.

Chapter Two

A FEW WORDS ABOUT the wardrobe—after my father's strategy of placing me in service of the family's common good succeeded, my mother stole a page from his book. The week after Father's pronouncement, she made multitudinous ones of her own. They included the following:

No daughter of hers would shame the family by wearing a widow's weeds shiny from overuse, especially when she wasn't a widow but a bereaved fiancée.

No daughter of hers would stay in a hotel or public pension.

And…

No daughter of hers would travel alone to San Francisco.

The first declaration led to a flurry of fittings and fabric purchases, after which she and Grandmother set to sewing, along with the housekeeper and any other female who could wield a needle.

Mercifully, I have always been an indifferent seamstress, something I pointed out to Mother when she tried to enlist me in this labor, reminding her, oh, so gently, that "no daughter of hers should shame the family" wearing suits with crooked hems and puckered seams. She accepted this truth with a silent scowl and went back to sewing.

On the second two points, I must admit the accommodations were to my liking. Mother exchanged letters with Mary Barton Granville, a family friend who lived near Nob Hill. She would take me in, quite happily, for however long I needed to stay in the city. She had a daughter, Abigail, who, though around ten years older than I, remained unmarried and would surely "enjoy company and a gentle influence." I looked forward to discovering the hidden meaning of that phrase.

My grandmother had helped tend to Mrs. Granville as a girl when her family had come west to settle in California. That family, the Bartons, was a faded memory to me, the elders having passed some time ago, and Mary—now Mrs. Granville—had moved to San Francisco when she married before I was born. Nonetheless, I had warm feelings for the family because of how my grandmother always spoke of them when she told me stories of her dramatic trip across the country so many years before. I knew them in spirit and looked forward to seeing Mary and her daughter in the flesh.

As to not traveling alone, well, here both Joe and I found pleasure in Mother's edict in this regard, though at first it had disturbed me, as I assumed Mother herself intended to be the traveling companion. But no, another, more amiable resolution prevailed.

Joe was sweet on a girl named Sally Tucker. Her family owned a spread in the southern part of the county, and Joe had let no opportunity pass to see her this past year, on the verge of actually keeping company with her. A kind, intelligent girl, Sally was planning on traveling north to visit her grandmother, who was ailing. We'd have to mind to each other during the journey. The Tuckers were relieved not to have to hire a chaperone for their daughter. I was relieved that the chaperone wasn't

Mother. And Joe was happy that Sally would be getting closer to his family.

Even with agreement on the broad outlines of the plan, small items still caused me to stumble in those weeks leading up to my exodus, irritations over how I should conduct our business, how I should disagree with the Southern Pacific agent while retaining his respect, how I shouldn't arrive at his office alone, if I could help it, and how to negotiate from a position of strength by not showing all my hand.

As my father tried to school me in these matters, I became snappish, frustrated that he did not appreciate my keen mind, once even stomping from his small study in anger.

In reality, I think I was trying to prove I could accomplish his task without it lessening my sorrow over my beloved's death one bit. Strange how this became part of my goal—to demonstrate to him that I'd stay true to my deceased fiancé despite whatever distractions he'd devise for me—but I set my mind to it as diligently as I set about learning the intricacies of Father's shipping needs.

And that, I realized as departure day approached, ended in victory…for him. Until this plan began taking shape, I'd not had to consciously remember my grief. It was as much a part of me as breathing, a daily soreness that made me sluggish and hurt.

But after my father assigned me this challenging task, I often had to wrestle my sadness to the forefront of my thoughts, reminding myself that, yes, I'd been loved by a good man and lost him. And, ironically, this caused a different sadness, a new parting, and a sorrowful resentment of those who'd take this pain that had become so dear away from me. I kept these feelings to myself. Or thought I did.

When I was most aware of my struggle to keep my grief alive, a sort of grumpy vexation would afflict me, igniting a strong impulse to argue with whomever was unlucky enough to be in my presence. More often than not, this was Father, as he led me through the intricacies of accounting and the records he'd compiled over the past few years.

He was cruelly patient with me, however, and I came to understand that my escalating irritation only fed his calm in these encounters, until I realized, in wonder, that he was, in fact, training me like a pet to crave his warmth, as I began quieting my tempestuousness to regain his soft affection.

He'd broken many spirited horses. Why should he not do the same with me?

By the time I was sufficiently outfitted and instructed for the journey north, I was also tamed. No longer did I look upon my parents as my enemies in my internal rupture over Miguel.

A battle might still rage in my heart, to be sure, but the warriors were all of my own making, loyalty to Miguel across the field from youth's natural desire to…live. I could not be placing Mother and Father on the battleground as hired substitutes. It wasn't fair. I had to war it out on my own.

SALLY WAS A GOOD companion, not one of those girls who felt the need to fill every silent moment with conversation, but one who knew a certain amount of talk would put us at ease with one another, let each of us know our limitations and our skills.

She wasn't sure, she told me on the train, that her grandmother was all that ill, but her parents seemed determined to get her away. She suspected it was because they feared she'd settle down too soon.

This bit of news, passed along to me with no guile or coy intent that I could see, set me to mulling its consequences for Joe. Were they afraid of her relationship with him?

"Not that I mind," she said, smoothing her soft tan suede gloves as the train pulled north, rattling and humming along the tracks. "I'm happy to have the opportunity to travel. I've heard San Francisco has an opera house, and I'm quite fond of music. I've also heard that one can find some fine silks and embroidered goods in Chinatown—going there with a companion, of course. We shall exchange addresses and stay in touch while in the city. I know our parents would want that."

I mused on this. She did seem eager to experience the big city. She didn't give the impression her jaunt would cause her one pang of pining for Joe, who I knew was already missing the chance to see her.

So, from this bit of information, I surmised my brother was in for disappointment. Her parents obviously knew of his interest and had packed her away to keep her out of love's reach. And she had not even been scraped by cupid's arrow deeply enough to express any yearning for the boy she was leaving behind. Poor Joe.

"That's a beautiful suit," she said, admiring the dark blue serge high-collared jacket and plain skirt I wore, the one newish outfit I'd had before the frenzied sewing session began. Mother had insisted I wear it with a small straw hat that seemed precariously pinned to my equally precariously styled hair, the locks secured in neat fulsome curls at the back of my head. It felt as if I had a pound of metal attached there—I'd better beware of any magnets—so many pins fastened the coif. On the ranch, I wore my hair down, tied at my nape.

Sally was similarly starched and "arranged," but she seemed more comfortable with it all. Her feathery golden hair stayed neat in a tight chignon, topped by a maroon felt hat matching her long jacket over a similar hued dress, the dark shades making her pale complexion milky white in contrast. I could see why Joe was taken with her. She was a beauty, and a vivacious one, alive with the desire to do things while she was young enough to enjoy them. I hoped he'd find another like her.

BY THE TIME we pulled into San Francisco, we both felt tired and worn. It made me wonder at the journey my grandmother had made more than a half century ago, by horse and foot across the country.

Being conveyed by this massive engine created a weariness all its own, though, as one's body still experienced the rigors of the long trip in some sped-up fashion, creating a series of aches that surprised you when you were least expecting such sensations.

Sally was immediately met at the station by a second cousin, Ralph, who shyly doffed his hat to us both, but whose gaze stayed true to Sally. While I could feel a curl or two of my hair straggling down my back, Sally managed to alight from the train as if she'd just had her toilette done by a lady's maid. She offered her hand to nervous Ralph, who didn't seem to know whether to kiss it or shake it. In the end, he gave it a cursory touch before making a show of looking for our bags.

When he found them, he again turned his attention to Sally. "Mother didn't say you were bringing your maid," he said, smiling. "But Grandmama has more than enough room to accommodate a whole passel of servants."

Sally blushed. I stormed. Of course he'd assume I was a maid, being dark of skin and hair. Before I could set him right—which would not have been a pleasant experience for him, I assure you—Sally shook her head and gently said, "You are mistaken, cousin. Ruth Sanchez is my traveling companion, and, I dare say, a new friend. She is here to visit with family friends while she conducts some business on behalf of her father, a leading rancher in the Carmel Valley."

Ralph, to his credit, apologized profusely and offered immediately to take me to Mrs. Granville's address. I forgave him but offered only stony silence as we took off for the Granville home.

We left the bustling station to find his buggy, and I breathed in the sensation of being in a big city for the first time.

The closest I'd come to this experience had been a few visits to Monterey, but that is a sleepy little village with charm and the slow pace of the tides.

This city was big and busy. People everywhere. Buildings that cut into the sky. Noise. Scents—not all of them pleasant. A faster rhythm. And strange single railroad cars, pulled by cables, gliding up and down hills!

I was unprepared, having heard only my grandmother's stories of this town when it had been little more than a few rows of buildings crammed up against the harbor. My, how it had grown. I found myself trying to memorize every new thing in order to write her about it later.

Sally and Ralph conversed during the ride, but I hardly listened to their jabber about weather and family. I was drinking in a new sensation—of being small and inconsequential. It made me want to be consequential, to make these people notice that I lived. I laughed.

"What is it, Ruth?" Sally inquired.

"Nothing, really," I said, waving the air in front of my face as the laughter came out again. "My father—I was thinking of how infuriating it is when he's right!"

At this, Sally laughed as well, knowing a bit of my own history that I'd shared on the train. Ralph smiled with no understanding.

I was soon delivered to Mary Granville's house, and Ralph deposited my bags for me at the door of what seemed to me a mansion of stone and brick, waiting with me until my ring was answered, making polite introductions of himself, and being on his way.

Mary Granville—what an impressive woman she was, tall, with dark hair streaked with gray, a long face that could look stern if her lips hadn't been impishly upturned at the corners, eyes that stared right through you, and a crisp, direct way of talking that delighted rather than offended.

"Come in, come in, my dear! I'm so glad you're here safe and sound. I'd never have guessed you as kin to Daniel and Kit Winchester! How exotic you are!" She hugged me so warmly that there was no question her comment held no sting. During the long embrace, I smelled her lavender perfume, a scent that took me back to Carmel and a lavender patch near the barn from which we'd pick blooms to dry for sachets. I felt a twinge of yearning for home and closed my eyes, letting it overtake me. It was as if I was letting Miguel back into my day, after I'd forcefully kept him out.

She ushered me into her well-furnished parlor, where she'd already had a maid place a silver platter of small treats—iced cakes and fruit, as well as a pitcher of what looked like lemonade. After asking if I'd like to freshen up—I assured her I was fine—we sat and she poured me a glass of the refreshing liquid. It soothed my travel-parched throat and revived me.

"I'm afraid Abigail is not here, but you will meet her this evening. We might also have a guest, I've been informed. Abigail often brings home people she meets through her work. I've learned to be resilient." She smiled and urged some cakes on me.

As I took one and began eating, she led our conversation into gentle pathways, inquiring about how I'd conduct my business, if I needed help, and then letting me know, just as Sally Tucker had done on the trip, various pieces of history so I wouldn't be distracted by wondering.

"My Alfred always felt a bit out of sorts in this house," she said, gesturing to the well-decorated room. It was crammed with ornate furniture, the walls hung with gilt-framed art and occasional family daguerreotypes. "He was a minister, you see, and we lived most of our life in more humble dwellings. But his parents bequeathed it to him, and we moved in rather than have his church pay for a parsonage. It was his intent to sell it and find modest accommodations, but he passed before that plan took shape. I will eventually put it up for sale, but I must admit I've grown comfortable here."

It was clear she battled her conscience over this, and I rushed to reassure her. "You're honoring your husband's parents by maintaining the household," I observed. "And you're providing employment for those who help you."

She smiled and tilted her head. "You'll do well with the Southern Pacific agent, my dear. You have a persuasive tongue." She laughed. "Your thoughts have been my own, but I wonder sometimes if I let comfort endorse my righteousness a little too much."

After more amiable talk, she showed me to my room, a large, sunny space on the back of the house, outfitted with four-poster bed, writing desk, armoire and more, much more formal than my plain room at the ranch, but comfortable nonetheless.

Dinner would be in an hour, she said, if Abigail managed to "straggle in" with her guest by then.

"You must be pleased at her dedication to the church," I said, naturally assuming she did charitable work at her late father's ministry.

Again, Mrs. Granville laughed. "I have no doubt that Abigail is a strong believer, but her church-tending is sometimes lax. No, her work is at the newspaper, and her hours irregular, which is why she is there today. She's a reportress."

A reportress? A job? A job that paid?

Left alone in the room, I pondered this, and with a shiver of excitement, I realized that I liked the idea of a woman working, not depending on a man for her sustenance and survival. Miguel, my beloved, was gone. I need not trouble my heart with finding a substitute. I could provide for myself, just as this Abigail Granville did. I looked forward to meeting her.

Chapter Three

THAT EVENING PROVED to be a momentous one, filled with drama, some of which, I must shamefully admit, amused me, as if I were watching a first-rate performance.

In my defense, some of it *was* performance, as Abigail Granville seemed to take great pleasure in goading her mother into colorful annoyance for the benefit of those of us who watched.

The "us" in this case included me, of course, and Abigail's guest—a handsome young man, recently arrived from the East—New York to be exact—whom she'd encountered when he was rummaging through old newspapers in the office "morgue" (which, Abigail explained to me, was the name they gave to the room that held old editions).

I'd planned on asking Abigail many questions about her job, in the hopes of gaining useful information about how one secured such a position, but that was not to be. She'd arrived barely in time for dinner, first of all, forestalling the possibility of polite conversation before the meal, and she'd made her entrance with such an extravagance of talk and activity that one hardly had the chance to get a word in edgewise. After our introductions—during which I just caught the gentleman's name—we were called into the dining room by Mrs. Granville and instructed to sit and eat before the soup was cold.

Immediately after being seated, Mrs. Granville said a short grace. I noticed Abigail reverently bowed her head and uttered a soft and sincere "amen" at the end. She did seem to have a strong spiritual side to her, despite her worldliness. After the prayer, Mrs. Granville spoke.

And then, it began…

"Oh, dear, Abigail, I fear I rushed you. I apologize. I should have allowed you some time to freshen up."

Abigail, spoon in midair, did not take offense. She raised her face and smiled charmingly and genuinely, deep dimples piercing her round cheeks. After slurping a sip off her spoon—which she did with a twinkle in her eye staring straight at her mother—she put her utensil down and found a stray lock of her abundant auburn hair, repinning it at the table, to her mother's obvious chagrin. She also looked down at her tan jacket lapel and gave it a perfunctory brush with her knuckles, an action that did nothing to remove a faint stain there.

Abigail was definitely not a woman who seemed to care much for her appearance. Although she was handsome in a rugged, outdoorsy sort of way, I had the impression she dressed not with appearance but with necessity in mind.

While this introductory act progressed, the male guest—Theodore was his first name, that much I'd caught during the whirlwind conversation at his and Abigail's arrival—looked from mother to daughter, his face a mask of growing concern as he seemed to contemplate what his appropriate reaction should be. Finally, chivalry won out over decorum, and he took Abigail's defense.

"Miss Granville is a pleasant sight to behold," he said with conviction. "I had not noticed anything amiss."

At this, both Mary Granville and her daughter paused, then laughed, which sent a blush raging over the poor man's face.

"I'm sorry, Theodore," Abigail said, "but that was so sweet."

"Very charming," her mother concurred. They'd both seen through his small disingenuousness. "But you don't need to feel compelled to take up for Abby. She's quite capable of defending herself, even when guilty."

"I did not feel compelled," Theodore said with growing uncertainty as he looked from one woman to the other. "I spoke the truth. Miss Granville is a singular beauty."

Then his gaze caught mine. I couldn't help myself. I, too, smiled at the poor fellow's position, caught between battling mother and daughter. I wanted to tell him to run off the field, one on which I, too, had been a warrior. My experience had taught me that casualties abounded when these conflicts arose.

He took my smile as something else, however, and immediately added, "I meant to say, of course, that all the women here are lovely—" he nodded at me, then looked straight into my eyes "—and I am a fortunate man to sit among such beauties."

Despite my amusement, my face warmed, touched by his sincerity. My "exotic" looks could have put off a lesser man who might have felt uncomfortable sitting at table with a *Californio*.

I looked down, suddenly embarrassed, as the conversation and the battle between mother and daughter continued.

"Well, Ruth here is certainly a beauty," Abby said. "I've no illusions about my own looks."

"Do not be so casual with your self disrespect," Mrs. Granville retorted. "You insult your ancestors, from whom you inherited those looks. That inheritance, of course, requires minding."

Abby snorted. "Honesty is no insult. And I do mind to how I look. I don't gad about buck naked, after all." She dove back into eating, as if famished.

"Hush, daughter. You make our guests uncomfortable."

"Well, then, let's shift the talk away from me," Abby said cheerfully, and turned her gaze toward me. "Mother tells me you are here on family business, Ruth."

I nodded, finishing my soup and touching the corners of my mouth with my napkin. "My father believes we are being overcharged by Southern Pacific. We ship fruits and vegetables, as well as sides of beef, north quite regularly."

"She lives on a ranch in Carmel Valley," Mary Granville interjected.

"Really?" Theodore sat up, interested. "Do you happen to know—"

Abby interrupted him, as if she didn't want him prying. "We shall have to help Ruth with strategy. The thieves at the railroad are quite powerful and shamefully corrupt. I've wanted to write about them for the paper, but my editor thinks those are stories better handled by…others. What do you suggest, Ted, is the best approach?"

"Do you know what the other ranchers are charged?" he asked me, his dark eyes penetrating and sharp. His good looks were subtle– a square, strong jaw, dark brown hair that seemed as untamable as Abigail's, a lean but muscular look about him.

"I'm afraid I don't have specific information on that, only a few stories my father has gathered from those ranchers willing to share. From this he's determined that perhaps the agents have been padding his bill."

"What would be their motive?" Mrs. Granville asked, quickly adding, "I mean, other than making more money. Why would they single out your father?"

"He's a good man," I hastened to say, "and perhaps too trusting."

Abigail's eyes narrowed. "You take after your father, I presume."

"Yes."

"Sad to say, but many a man is influenced by what he sees," Abigail said. "Seems our talk of looks is appropriate, after all, Mother. Men draw conclusions—often wrong ones—from appearances."

"Abigail!"

"Mother, I'm not blind. I've seen how people treat those who are different in looks from themselves. It is not heartening. The railroad agents probably treat her father unfairly because they think they can get away with bilking a man not of their own complexion."

Theodore sat, stunned by Abby's audacity. These were things that polite people did not discuss, especially among relative strangers. I, too, felt oddly unsettled, as if she'd revealed a deep family secret. Though I'd harbored the same thoughts—that the agents might be taking advantage of my father, assuming he was an unintelligent *Californio* or *Mestizo*, the word used to describe those of Mexican and Indian blood— I'd not confronted the idea outright. It was too…humiliating, and, yes, too wounding. My father's family had been in the valley for a long time, well before California had become a state or before Americans discovered our rich land. He had as much right—if not more—to claim citizenship and pride in his work. It was more than disheartening to think people capable of judging him poorly by the shade of his skin or his ancestry.

"You make our guests uncomfortable with such talk," Mrs. Granville said.

Just then, the maid came in to clear the table and provide the next course, a fragrant roast with fresh vegetables and biscuits. Once she had left, Abigail continued.

"As I said before, honesty is no insult. Nor should it be uncomfortable among the righteous." She smiled at Theodore and then at me. "And I always assume—until proven otherwise—that I am among the righteous."

"You have presumed the railroad agents are not," Mrs. Granville pointed out.

"But, Mother, have they not provided evidence against themselves—by overcharging Ruth's father, among the other ranchers, who they ostensibly treat fairly?" She pointed a fork at me.

"I think it's not helpful to fill Ruth's head with resentment when no one yet knows what the true story might be."

Theodore cleared his throat and spoke. "I have to agree with Miss Granville, I'm afraid. Her assumption is not unreasonable since evidence exists of wrongdoing."

"Ted studied the law," Abby said, as if this settled things.

As for me, I listened raptly, my mood changing throughout the talk from frozen embarrassment to resolute determination. Abby had articulated my darkest thoughts, thoughts I was sure my father shared but would never have passed along to me. It was better to face these notions and be done with them, one way or another. Honesty is no insult, Abby had said. She was right. The truth made me stronger.

"Let's talk of happier things," Mrs. Granville suggested. "Caruso, the Italian tenor of great repute, is visiting the city soon."

"Opera always seemed like caterwauling to me, I'm afraid," Abby said. "But it will certainly be good for the city to have such a prestigious visit."

"Opera is quite moving," Theodore said, in a voice that indicated he was glad to be on more neutral ground. "I have been quite often in New York. Have you ever been, Miss Sanchez?"

I shook my head. "No, but I'm fond of music generally."

"Then perhaps we should all go," Mrs. Granville suggested. "I will purchase the tickets as a treat."

"That is too generous," Theodore said. "I should be the one offering the treat."

"Don't be silly, Theodore," Abby interjected. "You've hardly an extra penny to spare. Mother can easily handle it." Noticing his discomfort at her disclosure of his personal finances, she added, "The trip west was expensive, I'm sure. Until you get on your feet here, you should be thrifty."

Mrs. Granville smiled and shook her head.

Abigail gave her a sharp look. "What have I done now?"

Before they could resume hostilities, I said, "I've heard so much about opera and about Mr. Caruso's magnificent voice. It will be wonderful to hear him. I can hardly wait to write and tell my parents."

The dinner proceeded thus, with eddies of polite conversation sometimes overtaken by waves of outspoken comments from Abby, followed by equally fierce waves of rebuke from her mother. Once I knew what to expect, I enjoyed myself. Except for a few more moments where Abby's obsession with "honesty" flowed toward impudence, it was a pleasant dinner, much livelier than the quiet meals we shared at the ranch back home.

However, after we'd finished our coffee and retreated to the parlor, I could hardly keep my eyes open, something that both Granville women noticed. They insisted I would not offend should I want to retire, so I left them as they sat down to converse more with Theodore, who, I noted, seemed disappointed by my departure.

As I rounded the corner to the staircase, I heard the following exchange, which darkened Mrs. Granville's voice and mood considerably, it seemed to me:

"I'm embarrassed to admit that I did not catch your full name," Mrs. Granville said, and I paused to hear so I could learn it, as well.

"Theodore Crane Beaumont."

"Crane?" Mrs. Granville repeated, uneasily. "Of course, that's a common name." This was more to herself than to her guests.

"His mother was a Crane," Abby said. "That's why he's here. We might as well air the story. He wants to help his grandfather."

"Not—"

"William Crane, Mrs. Granville," Theodore said softly and sadly. "You and your parents, the Bartons, might have known him long ago as Billy."

Chapter Four

OH, HOW I LONGED to hear more, but I was too afraid of being found out as an eavesdropper and too tired to rejoin the group. I also had the impression that Abigail had deliberately waited until I was gone to start this talk about Theodore's mission. It troubled me. Who was Billy Crane?

A common name, but a familiar one. As I tended to my evening toilette, unpinning and brushing my hair, washing the day's grime and dust from face and body, changing into my comfortable white cotton nightshirt, I turned the name over in my head.

If Mary Barton Granville knew the man from long ago, if her parents, the Bartons, had known him, as Theodore had suggested, then perhaps it had been from her days in Carmel with her father, Josephus, and her mother, Willa? Or maybe even before that, on the trail west, when my grandmother and grandfather had made the journey.

I sat at a small desk by the window, determined to stay awake long enough to pen a short letter to Mother and Father to post in the morning. I knew they'd worry about me, and I wanted to assure them I'd arrived safely and now had a strong shoulder—Abigail's—upon which to lean should I need help in my endeavors.

As I wrote my short letter, a memory came back to me of my grandmother answering my brother's questions about life on the trail. He'd asked her if there had been any dangerous Indians, and she'd replied, no, the Indians didn't trouble them, but some bad men had. He'd pressed for more, thrilled to hear an adventurous tale. All she would say was "Billy Crane was one. But he's gone to justice by now, I'm sure."

Billy Crane. It had to be the same man if Mary Granville had known of him, as well.

I quickly penned a postscript: "Mother, did grandmother ever talk to you about a Billy Crane? His grandson is here in the city, and Abigail Granville knows him."

Not knowing the full story, I didn't say more, didn't tell her I'd supped with the man's grandson.

Previously drowsy, I was now awake with that restless energy that afflicts you when you have had a tiring day but are eager to face the next new excitement. I sat at the desk, looking dreamily at the moon out the window, hung in the sky like a mesmerizer's medallion.

Such a jumble of feelings washed over me. Happiness, yes. I'd enjoyed meeting Abigail and witnessing her cheerful battle with her mother. It gave me heart, knowing that one could disagree with one's mother and still show such love. I'd been sure to include loving words to my own mother in the letter I'd just written.

I also felt a strange, tugging sadness, as I wished I could share this adventure with my Miguel. I remembered how I'd thought of him when entering this household, how it had comforted me to think of him.

But when I imagined him sharing these new experiences with me—on the train with me, or in the Granville's dining room—something seemed out of place and uncomfortable. He'd been a man of the open spaces. He'd loved ranching. He'd enjoyed our simple life in Carmel Valley. He'd not even enjoyed going into Monterey all that often. And he'd sometimes felt ill at ease at my family's table, making the smallest of small talk, just enough not to be rude.

Honesty is no insult, Abigail had said. To be honest, Miguel would not have enjoyed this adventure nearly as much as I was now. Honesty is no betrayal, either, I assured myself. I could still cherish his memory.

But his memory seemed as far away as home on this first night of my San Francisco adventure, and that made me miss him, but in a curious way. I missed the part of me that had felt so completely in union with him. It seemed to be pulling apart and away.

Soon, even these troubling thoughts were not enough to keep Morpheus from my door. I lay on the soft bed and promptly fell asleep.

I'D LOOKED FORWARD to the next day—Sunday—as a day for rest, but it turned out to be tiring, if also pleasantly social. After accompanying the Granvilles to church, we came home to an afternoon of visits. At church, Mrs. Granville had invited several friends and acquaintances to stop by and meet me. For several hours, it felt as though a house party was in full sway with me as the center of attention. Every time I turned around, Mrs. Granville was introducing me to someone, and I was peppered with questions about life in the valley on a ranch. Even though the housekeeper, Stella, was off that day, Mrs. Granville, with Abby's help and my attempts to pitch in, managed to make sure every guest was fed and properly tended.

At first, I inwardly rebelled at the activity. I wasn't used to being the center of attention. In fact, I'd shunned that role entirely during my mourning for Miguel. And I was ashamed to admit that for a brief moment or two I'd wondered if Mrs. Granville had conspired with my mother to yank me into the world by bringing the world to me.

It was impossible, however, to retain that irritation when the Granvilles were so friendly and cheerful, and Mrs. Granville so obviously proud to show off this friend of the family, a link to her parents' past.

But it was that past I was now eager to hear more of—specifically, the past involving Ted's grandfather. There was no time to pursue such conversations with them, though, as the day wore on.

And, when the last guest left, the Granvilles all but collapsed in comfortable chairs in the parlor, reading and dozing. I couldn't upset that repose with nosy and possibly unsettling questions. My interrogation would have to wait another day.

TWO THINGS DISTURBED me in the morning. First, I awoke afraid I would have missed seeing Abigail before she left for the day—Mrs. Granville had let me sleep in. And second, I'd dreamed about Theodore Beaumont.

As I tried to pin up my hair and make myself presentable, my hands shook. I attributed it to my rush— Mrs. Granville had informed me when I'd poked my head into the hallway earlier that Abigail had not left yet and would wait for me—but I knew in my heart that I was disturbed by that dream, the memory of which had left a faint impression on my senses, like a footprint on sand.

I'd dreamt that Theodore Beaumont had accompanied Sally Tucker and me to San Francisco, and when he'd shown interest in her, I became jealous, even to the point of anger. I awakened from that dream feeling both embarrassment and remorse.

How silly! I'd just met the man. It must have been my confusing thoughts about Miguel last night that had muddled my heart.

I shook my head and hurried downstairs, racing into the dining room where Abigail sat at the far end of the table, sipping what smelled like strong coffee. She smiled at me and pointed to the sideboard, on which were laid out fruits and toast, some sausages and eggs.

"Mother has already eaten. She's getting ready to leave for church," she told me as I filled my plate. "She does charitable work several times a week." She smiled at me as I sat down, and I was struck by how open her face was, filled with good-natured intent.

I was also struck by the fact that, although it was morning and she'd just dressed, she still had the air of someone who'd been out and about, her coif tussled, her dress careless. Although her hair was pulled up in a small bun, tendrils draped the sides of her face like wind-blown sheers. She wore a different suit from the day before—this one a berry hue—but the collar was half turned in on itself. Seeing my gaze go there, she reflexively fixed it without even a hint of self-consciousness.

"I'm glad we have some time to talk," I began, as I sat near her. "I would enjoy hearing more about the work you do." I also wanted to learn more about Theodore and his grandfather, but I didn't think it polite to jump into that.

I needn't have feared this line of conversation. Before she had a chance to respond, Mrs. Granville strode in the room, pulling on her gloves.

"I'm sorry I can't be with you today, Ruth," she said. "But Abby will be happy to help you with your first appointments." After checking her hat in the mirror above the sideboard, she quickly added, "And, Abby, be sure to tell her about Mr. Crane—"

"Beaumont, Mother," Abby said softly. "His name is Beaumont."

"Yes, well—I don't want her parents getting word of this…situation…without her being fully informed." Standing tall and straight, she added, "Please try not to be late for supper."

"I won't, Mother. Goodbye."

After Mrs. Granville left, I looked at Abby expectantly, waiting for her to tell the story, relieved that I didn't need to pry, eager to hear a good tale. She wasted no time.

"Ted's grandfather is in San Quentin, and he's come to clear his name before he's wrongly executed." She stood and refilled her coffee cup, as if the news wasn't startling. But, of course, she'd had time to absorb it, while it was fresh to me. Billy Crane had been a "bad man" along the trail during my grandparents' journey west and now was slated for execution. A chill went through me. "Why don't you tell me how much you know about his grandfather before I go on?"

"Only that my grandparents thought he was…well, they didn't think highly of him," I said, trying to be polite.

Abby guffawed. "Don't be so kind. He was a thief and a drinker, a criminal of the lowest sort. Even Ted says so. Mother knows the story because she had faint memories of being warned to stay away from him on the trail west, and at one point, when she was a girl in the valley, they became afraid that he was on the loose there. It turned out to be a false alarm, but her mother—my grandmamma Willa—told her the whole sordid tale. Mother said it's a good thing her younger brother, my uncle William, lives in Montana now, or he'd be heading to San Quentin to do the man in himself, after hearing the family stories about him!"

And Abby told me those "family stories" now. Billy Crane had been on the wagon train west with my grandparents. He'd apparently made advances to my grandmother, which my grandfather had stopped. But when Billy Crane's brother had died in a river crossing, Billy had blamed my grandfather and ultimately shot him, almost killing him. If this weren't bad enough, the man had tried to set up my grandmother for a kidnapping in San Francisco. She was rescued with the help of my grandfather, who'd recovered from his wounds.

My eyes widened as I heard the tale. My grandparents had regaled me with stories of the trail, but never this one in such detail. When I mentioned this, Abby just shook her head.

"They probably thought it too rough a story for young ears," she said. "I wouldn't be surprised if your mother doesn't even know all of it."

I thought of the letter to my mother in which I'd mentioned Billy Crane. It sat on a silver tray in the foyer awaiting posting. I wondered if it would cause a stir back home, with Mother asking Grandmother for a fuller account. For a moment, I thought of retrieving it, but remembered Abby's words: Honesty is no insult. The truth about the past shouldn't be able to hurt my loved ones any longer. Of course, the past's tentacles were reaching out to touch us since Crane's grandson, Theodore, was here. But I'd not mentioned much about him in the letter.

"Anyway, Billy Crane might have been a rascal in his day, but he's old and reformed now, according to Ted. He wanted nothing to do with the bad life he'd left behind, but he was charged with murder and robbery—a group of men in the hills—five months ago. He'll hang for it."

"Murder! Of…several men?" My eyes narrowed, and I had to admit I had my doubts about how reformed the man was and whether Ted wasn't letting family loyalty blind him to the truth.

"I know what you're thinking because I thought it, too," Abby said. "But Ted is sure his grandfather is innocent—of this crime, at least— because he has an alibi. Someone was with him at the time of the crime, someone who can vouch for him. Besides, the only witness to the deed itself was another prospector whose drinking put him in the grave shortly after the crime was committed. He was unreliable at best, claiming Mr. Crane acted with one or two others, but because of Billy Crane's record, this didn't matter to a jury."

"If his grandfather has an alibi, then what's the problem?"

Abby sighed and nibbled on some toast. "He can't be found. Mr. Crane apparently had gone wandering—his reformation included a conversion, or rather, a return to the faith of his youth. He'd decided to set about a 'journey into the wilderness' to cleanse his body and his soul, to steal away from temptation, to meditate and pray."

"And that's where he encountered this other man?"

"Yes. He says it was a traveling preacher."

I couldn't help it. I laughed. It seemed so preposterous. Abby laughed, too.

"I know, I know. It does make you wonder. But Mr. Crane says the man prayed with him, blessed him, offered him advice—including setting things right with those he'd offended—and then was on his way. He didn't get a last name. Just called him 'Preacher John.' And he has a description. Tall, long white hair, very thin, limps a little, and a scar like a half moon on his upper lip."

"And Mr. Beaumont intends to find this man?" I asked, incredulous.

Before Abby could respond, someone else did:

"Yes, I do. And please, call me Ted."

I'd not heard the front door open, so I was shocked when he entered the room, my heart fluttering in my chest like a caged bird, my hand rattling the coffee cup so that it fell to the floor. He bent and retrieved it, placing it out of reach.

"Here, I'll get you a fresh cup," he said. "I'm sorry I startled you."

"I hope you don't mind," Abby said to me, "but I told Ted to come by this morning. Although Mother's not too happy about this adventure, she won't put any obstacles in front of it. She gave me the names of several pastors to consult about our mystery minister." She looked at Ted. "Please, help yourself. You might as well fortify yourself now, in case we have a long search in front of us."

"You're very kind, Abby, but I didn't realize Miss Sanchez would be here when you offered to help me last night. I only came to tell you I'd be moving along on my own. You have Miss Sanchez's business to attend to."

Although this seemed a chivalrous gesture, to put my business above his own, it annoyed me. I'd already seen that Abigail's spirit relished the mystery his grandfather's case presented. I would not let him use my assignment to keep Abby from the challenge she'd surely enjoy more.

"No, Mr. Beaumont—"

"Ted."

"—Ted, I insist that we both help you with your endeavor. A man's life is at stake in your case. A few dollars in mine." I'd take care of my father's business later today or even tomorrow—on my own, with my own wits as weapons.

"She's got you there," Abby said. "Besides, you're a lawyer. You can help intimidate those Southern Pacific vultures with your very presence. We can stop there during the day, and I expect to hear a symphony of Latin phrases flowing from those well-educated lips as we stand in their offices setting Ruth's family business to rights."

"I would be happy to be of use in such a manner."

"Really," I said, my face flushing, "I had fully intended on handling it by myself. I've prepared for the meeting. My father placed his trust in me." And his respect. I intended to show him he'd been wise to do so.

"As well he should have," Abby said. "But I'm sure Ted here will be a tremendous aid in your mission, even if he just stands in a corner and glares at the agents."

Ted nodded and smiled. "I can be very effective at glaring, if that is what will do the job."

I remembered my father's suggestion that I not go alone to the railroad office if I could help it. I'd planned on asking Abby to accompany me, but it was clear she'd insist Ted go, too.

"All right," I said "You may accompany me."

Still a bit put out by his sly arrogance, and equally annoyed that I'd yet had time to talk with Abby alone about her employment, I remained polite but not loquacious during the rest of breakfast. Ted did end up joining us, feasting on every delectable the housekeeper had placed out for us, even going for seconds, so that it was nearly two hours before we were finally on our way.

As we were going out the front door, he smiled at me. "I neglected to mention that you look even more beautiful in the sunshine than you did by candlelight. That green color becomes you very much. May I call you Ruth?"

I warmed with blush, or maybe it was ire. Although I did think the sage green dress I'd chosen set off my eyes and hair, there was something about his compliment that made it seem more like goad than praise.

"I'll think on it," was all I said, brushing past him.

Chapter Five

I DID QUITE A BIT of thinking that day, and most of it was unsettling.

We started our day with a cable car ride—my first ever, one that left me breathless with excitement and nervousness, too, listening to the creaks and crackles of wheels being pulled up angled hills. I thought it would feel like the train ride to San Francisco, but it was more open and more immediate, the road just a glance away, the hills impossibly steep so that I held my breath as we crested them, then gasped again as we descended the next incline. I disliked the feeling of powerlessness. On a horse, I was able to control the journey.

Ted made conversation the entire time, but I suspected he did it to try to calm me, which ended up making me all the more aware of my womanly fragility. I'd ridden—even broken—some strong, spirited horses. How dare he assume I was nervous—even if I was? I just wished he would be quiet and let me experience and conquer my fear on my own.

I tolerated, even tried to look cheery during his questions about my father's ranch, how much acreage we owned, how we sold our goods. But I couldn't help thinking that my strained answers, sometimes uttered in a thin voice while I looked out the window and not at Ted, gave more away about my fears than covered them up, making me resentful of his desire to keep me talking. Just leave me be, I mentally shouted. Let me bear this in silence. It was insufferable to have to go through this torment with an audience.

Abigail, I noticed, was calm as a nesting bird, sitting comfortably near a window and staring at the view. I envied her the silence. Why didn't Ted talk to her?

When we disembarked near the Southern Pacific offices, Ted offered his hand and, wouldn't you know it, I stumbled as I stepped down, causing me to lean into him, grabbing his strong shoulders as I righted myself.

Why, I must have appeared a fragile stumblebum! I couldn't stop thinking he'd helped engineer this impression with his constant prattle and garrulous desire to aid me. I needed to collect my thoughts, to be ready for the railroad agents.

Then, when we went into the Southern Pacific office, before I could even open my mouth, he was talking again!

In his defense, the man who greeted us, Mr. Jenkins, immediately assumed Ted was the person in charge of our little group, but still…Ted spoke so fast and so much I couldn't even begin to utter a word. Just when I thought I should start my negotiation, Ted pulled the rug out from under me by introducing Abigail and myself as "gentle ladies whose business required the services of a legal nature and who were accompanying him as representatives of their respective families who, while unwilling to present themselves to the rail company on their own, were highly respected and capable of financing a multitude of deals."

He then turned to me and surprised me by speaking a phrase in Spanish: *Please respond in this language. Say anything.*

I complied with a torrent, telling him this hadn't been my plan, that I was capable of handling this on my own and would do so if he stopped this ridiculous charade and observing that I didn't enjoy being treated as an imbecile.

He merely said, again in Spanish, "*Si, si*. I understand you a little. My Spanish is not that good. Let him think you are not wise. It is good, no?"

At this, he smiled broadly, and before I could respond, he turned to our host again while nodding soberly in our direction as if we'd given him instructions he was merely affirming, and adding, "They will be silent during our negotiations, but do not let that mislead you into the false assumption that their passivity means they are *non compos mentis* because I can assure you they are superior intellects, a challenge to the notion that women's small brains make them unsuitable for higher decisions. I could not perform this duty on their family's behalf, in fact, were they not present—*res ipsa loquitor*, they are here to reassure their brethren that I am performing my task with all due diligence and, *mutatis mutandi*, will, I am sure, give a suitable account of today's transactions before any final decisions are made. Do you understand?"

Ted smiled broadly. Abigail stared coldly, acting the part, while Mr. Jenkins, the hapless agent, a man of stout proportions and ruddy complexion, looked bewildered as he tried to appear accommodating.

As to my expression, I was aflame with indignation. I'd specifically told Ted I would handle things, and now he was taking over without consulting me at all! I had a mind to stop this ridiculous show, but I was smart enough to realize that would demonstrate weak disorganization, putting me at a disadvantage. I'd have to wait out this intolerable drama and then clean up the wreckage later.

Oh, I'd give Ted a piece of my mind about that, too! As I stood there, I could barely contain myself, my foot tapping to an unheard beat, my glare as angry as a mother bear's whose cubs have been threatened. My glare—I was the one in the position of glaring, when we'd specifically said, or rather, Abby had suggested, that Ted be the one with that role!

Ted was now spewing a veritable fountain of unctuous compliments to Mr. Jenkins, so exaggerated as to be patently untrue, but Mr. Jenkins seemed all too happy to sop them up and then to talk to us—or rather, to Ted—when Ted inquired about multiple shipping contracts for a "variety of well-to-do clients who wish to remain anonymous" –this delivered with a knowing wink in our direction—until he'd gathered "sufficient information" to quell their doubts about using the train for transport. We were clearly meant to be the representatives of these clients.

With such an enticement, we were ushered into a back office, Abigail and I exchanging glances, hers giving nothing away. Perhaps she was as uncomfortable as I was with subterfuge. I preferred to attack our problem with no chicanery. Direct accusation, interrogation and resolution were what I'd had in mind. I was sure I'd have a chance to use them once Ted was finished with his playacting.

"Please, sit down." Mr. Jenkins fussed about us, pulling over an extra chair so that we all three could face him. But Ted grabbed the heavy wooden seat from the man and placed it close to the desk, sitting there himself while Abigail and I took the ones farther away, to the side and slightly in back of Ted. "I apologize that I have no tea or other refreshment to offer you." He glanced at us.

The room was paneled but not dark. Drawings of trains and rail track through countryside adorned the walls. A cuspidor sat discreetly in the corner, while a humidor with cigars was within hand's reach on the otherwise clear desk. The sweet-musty smell of old cigar smoke hung lightly in the room.

"So, er, tell me some more about these…clients of yours, Mr. Beaumont," Mr. Jenkins began, wiping his brow with a handkerchief and glancing at us again. Poor man. I actually felt sorry for him. Such a waste of his time! After Ted failed, Mr. Jenkins might actually be eager to deal directly with me. "I have shipping rates tables here and all our coastal corridor schedules. Of course, we're eager to work out special deals with customers who guarantee a certain amount of cargo, particularly if it involves amounts over various levels. We can even schedule special trains—although that is a bit more expensive—for regular runs, of course…."

He handed Ted several papers he'd pulled from a drawer, and I was flabbergasted by the amount of time Ted took to study them. Minutes ticked by as he pored over the pages, nodding his head occasionally, twisting his mouth into worried confusion other times, once asking Mr. Jenkins for a pencil which he used to jot notes on a paper—also requested from Mr. Jenkins—while he studied, studied, studied.

Every time Mr. Jenkins sought to interrupt this meticulous analysis with an observation or additional information, Ted would hold up a finger indicating he needed silence to continue his work.

I looked at Abigail to see if she were as exasperated with this performance as I was, but her face was stonily impassive, giving away not one clue of what she was really thinking. Just when I couldn't stand another second and was about to speak up, Ted glanced quickly at me before addressing Mr. Jenkins.

"Aha, I see now. Yes, yes, this makes perfect sense," Ted said at last. But this was not the end of this scene. Oh, no. He passed the schedules and rate tables along to Abigail—a wise choice since I would have been too tempted to let loose my inner fury had they come to me—while continuing to calculate items on his scrap of paper.

For her part, Abigail copied the spirit of Ted's role-playing, perusing the pages as if they were long-lost codex to a buried treasure or ancient manuscript. I sat, stunned, now growing increasingly impatient with this nonsensical act. My foot was tapping again.

Ted must have sensed my restlessness because as Abigail continued her reading, he began to speak softly.

So softly, in fact, that it took me several moments to realize he was no longer putting on a show but finally addressing the subject I'd come here to handle. He started by asking about a contract for an amount of goods that aligned perfectly with the numbers I'd provided him on the trolley about my father's business. He'd not been making small talk to make me feel comfortable, after all. He'd been gathering information.

In stunned silence and with burning realization, I listened as he described a possible contract whose details dovetailed precisely with my father's dealings. At the end of Ted's serious presentation, Mr. Jenkins smiled broadly and announced an amount that he was sure would be accurate "since this is precisely the kind of deal we make with numerous farmers and ranchers every day."

Then Ted looked worried. He frowned. He rubbed his chin. He opened his mouth to speak, then closed it.

"What can I help you with, sir?" Mr. Jenkins asked politely. "You seem to be puzzling with something. I'm sure we can explain it."

Ted didn't look up but pointed at his paper, upon which he'd scribbled numerous figures and tallies.

"I hope so, Mr. Jenkins. Because I'm afraid I must be making some sort of miscalculation."

And then, his voice changed. It became hard steel encased in soft velvet, low but unwavering. He looked Mr. Jenkins directly in the eye and proceeded to tell him that the figures Mr. Jenkins was quoting were nothing like those a certain client was already paying, a client whose daughter was in this very room, and whose father was a well-connected ranch owner whose ancestors had helped carve prosperity out of California's bountiful land.

"I'm sure if this client of mine knew of these lower rates, he would not be considering alternative transportation—shipping, for one—that he might also be recommending to the ranchers up and down the rail lines. His word is valued, you should know, since his family has long resided in the valley. He holds a great deal of influence. It would be hard if it came to that, wouldn't it, Mr. Jenkins?" Ted asked impassively. "To lose so much business because of an error in arithmetic?"

Mr. Jenkins's faced turned red and seemed to swell. Perspiration beaded on his brow and cheeks as he fumbled, verbally and physically, to make things right. He searched his desk for record books and found the appropriate one, while Ted calmly gave him my father's name, pronouncing it with the correct accent. He murmured that he wasn't sure why there had been a problem, that he was sure the company could rectify it.

I had the immense satisfaction of seeing his jaw practically hit the floor when I broke my silence and uttered what I hoped was a charming "Thank you for your help." He clearly had thought I spoke no English. Ted's eyebrows lifted, as if he was unsure my revelation was a good thing, but he quickly smiled, as if this were all part of his grand scheme.

By the time we left, Ted had secured a contract in writing and a promise to stay on top of this particular client's needs.

Out in the cool air, we stared at each other, Abigail fairly bursting to say something. But Ted shook his head ever so slightly and strolled with us several blocks before he let us speak. I was a swirling mix of emotion— gratitude for Ted's help in fixing my problem but a dark cloud of anger for how he'd done it.

"There, ladies, we are safely away from that hawk's lair. Perhaps we should stop for some refreshment."

Abigail commenced laughing, a giggle bubbling up into a hearty chuckle, infectious in its joy. And, despite my irritation and rage, I found a smile teasing my lips as I shared Abby's enjoyment of the moment.

"Oh, Ted, the Latin—thank you for that!" Abby managed to say between laughs. "It was a wonderful performance. Who needs to see Caruso after such a beautiful act?"

"Really, it was no act," he said, grinning now in the light of Abigail's compliments. "I spoke not a false word."

At this, Abby snorted. "Well-to-do clients?"

"But that was truth, plain and simple. Ruth's father is well-to-do in comparison to others less fortunate, and you, Abby, are surely considered in the same class."

"And has nothing – no goods – to ship whatsoever," I chided, my original irritation returning.

"Not at the moment, no. But one never knows where fortune will take one," he mused. "I was merely giving voice to aspirations. And, I might add, that I, too, am grateful that you both complied with my implied admonition to be silent."

"I had to bite my cheeks," Abby said. "I think they're bleeding!"

"Then let's find some balm for them. Perhaps a silky soup from Beddinger's around the corner here." He offered me his arm, but I didn't take it.

Chapter Six

THROUGHOUT OUR MEAL of oysters and veal chops, I was of a mixed mind. It was impossible not to share in Abby's mirth as she went over, point by point, Ted's performance in the railroad agent's office. Despite my irritation, I found myself smiling, even laughing, as Abby recounted the escapade so we could relive it together.

But Ted had assumed that I myself could not handle the action, and that still made me angry, something he began to sense as the luncheon went on.

"Ruth, I'm afraid I offended you in some way with my performance," he said softly. "That was not my intent. I apologize if my manner was not to your liking."

Even this apology enflamed me! He seemed so condescending about it, as if my "liking" was the issue, not his...his arrogance!

"I was sent here by my father to handle his business," I said with steely softness. "So I was naturally surprised when you took it upon yourself—with no consultation beforehand—to act as my agent."

Abby's eyebrows shot up, but she remained silent.

Ted nodded and leaned toward me. "You're right. I'm sorry. I assumed wrongly that you wanted me to help, to use my legal skills, that is...."

"Oh, it was my fault," Abby hastily interjected. "I was the one encouraging him to spout off in Latin—

which was wonderful, Ted, really wonderful! Don't hold it against him, Ruth. As usual, I'm the one sticking my nose in when I shouldn't have. I'm sure you would have done just as good a job with the agent."

"Yes, I agree," Ted said. "I denied you the opportunity. I apologize again. You might even have done a better job."

I stared at them both across the table from me, so eager to be in my good graces again. Sitting ramrod straight, I felt blush creep up my neck. How ungrateful I must look to them! Ted had just done me an enormous good deed, yet I had managed to push him to say he was sorry for it!

"Please, do not apologize. I should be the one offering my regret—I never thanked you sufficiently for helping me, Ted. Let me show my gratitude by paying for our luncheon."

At that, Ted stiffened. Like most men, he'd not enjoy having a woman treat him.

"Well, I...I am perfectly capable of paying...." he mumbled. "And I didn't expect any payment from you for my...my..."

"Your performance," I said, "which, as Abby said, was magnificent. But really, I insist. Please, order what you like. I have sufficient funds for a feast! I insist. Really." I must admit that it gave me pleasure to see him squirm a little at my offer. Now he knew how I'd felt, accepting his uninvited favor.

His eyes met mine, and I swear I saw in them recognition and understanding. A soft smile lifted his lips, and he held up his tea cup.

"I'm not a drinking man, but if I were, I'd offer this toast," he said. "To women—never underestimate their intelligence."

"Hear, hear!" Abby said with enthusiasm.

Past this rocky start, we had such a fine time at Berringer's that we spent nearly the rest of the day there. After Abby and Ted—and now, even I—again went over the railroad agent incident, we moved on to more mirth as Ted regaled us with stories of his law studies, during which he apparently was quite the scalawag, getting away with as little work as possible, and pulling pranks and engaging in all kinds of tomfoolery while at the university. It was clear he'd had practice with chicanery.

At first, I found myself disapproving. His stories presented a somewhat unflattering portrait of him, after all. And my Miguel had been serious about his work— you'd never have found him trying to get out of a task or taking it lightly. But Ted's love of life and good sport was so infectious—and I had to remind myself that I certainly wasn't the type of girl to frown like a schoolmarm on innocent fun—that it didn't take long before I was giggling along with Abby at his shenanigans.

I laughed at his engaging stories, yes, but I became wary of such a reckless personality, as well, judging him suitable for an afternoon's entertainment but not a lasting friendship. That comforted me, in an odd way, making me feel as if I was not giving up on Miguel, that I was safe from other attractions. How strange.

But then he shared a sad story, his voice going low, just as it had in the railroad agent's office when he'd finally gotten around to the true nature of our visit.

"Alas, those freewheeling days abruptly came to a halt six months prior to my graduation. My mother passed away." He looked down, fidgeting with the corner of his linen napkin. I swallowed, not knowing what to say. Abby reached over and clutched his hand.

"Oh, dear, Ted. I'm so sorry. I didn't know."

He looked up and pasted a smile on his face that was as false as his airs had been hours ago. "You needn't be sorry. We met only a day ago. And losing one's parent is not a singular bit of news. You, yourself, have experienced such loss."

"But immediately before your graduation? That must have been a blow," I said softly, thinking of how happily I'd anticipated my marriage to Miguel, only to have it stolen from me by his passing. It seemed to me that grief was more painful when coupled with such simple disappointments.

"Ruth is right," Abby added. "When my father passed on, it was after a good, full life in which he'd seen me grow up and secure a position at the newspaper. I wasn't deprived of the warmth from that parental pride as you were. And although I do miss my father, I have the satisfaction of knowing he'd been able to witness and take pleasure in my accomplishments."

"Your sympathy is touching, and I thank you," he said, looking from one of us to the other. "I have sought to redeem myself by being a strong protector and support to my younger sister, Elizabeth Ann."

"I didn't realize you had a sister," Abby commented. "Is she here in the city with you? We must invite her over!"

"No, she is still back in New York, although I do wish she could meet you both. She'd benefit from your companionship, I'm sure. Elizabeth is a timid girl, a pure and gentle spirit. She misses our mother terribly, and we have no other relatives close enough to help."

"Your father…" I began, unsure of whether I should pry.

"Passed on before we were old enough to know him. A great-uncle set up a trust fund for Mother, which she used to care for us. Unfortunately, we found it was nearly gone at the time of her death. She'd started using principle several years before…" He stopped and blinked, clearly moved by the story he was telling, as if he'd not confided it to anyone before. My heart ached for him, and, without thinking, I placed my hand over his on the table.

"Please, you needn't go on. It is clearly a painful tale, and we shouldn't have pressed you for details," I said. Especially when those details painted a picture of a sweet, indulgent mother who couldn't say no to her lively son, thus ruining her future and theirs in the process. No wonder Ted was troubled telling us this story. He felt guilty, the poor soul. But he shouldn't—he hadn't known.

"My plan is to become a successful attorney and support my sister in the way to which she became accustomed." He squeezed my hand gently. It was warm and sent a prickle through my skin.

"But surely you're not being paid to clear your grandfather," Abby said. "That is an act of mercy."

He paused, obviously thinking of how to phrase his next revelation. "I will admit to being motivated first and foremost by the pressing plight of a man facing the gallows. But I will also confess to baser objectives. If I do prove my grandfather's innocence, my reputation will be made."

"There is no shame in that!" Abby said forcefully, and I found myself nodding my head in agreement. "If you are successful, you should feel no remorse in reaping a just reward from it—the reward of acclaim."

"I agree," I said. "I have little patience with false humility. If you win your grandfather's suit, you should not have to pretend that you don't deserve whatever good comes your way."

He gave me a strained look, which I interpreted once again to mean we had trod too close to personal matters. I started to apologize but couldn't find the appropriate words. Something about Ted Beaumont unnerved me, and fast on the heels of his confessions came unease..

Why? My face warmed, and I looked down.

AFTER FINISHING WITH some extravagant berries and cream, we walked all the way back to the Granville household. Abby insisted we stroll instead of taking the trolley or another conveyance. I think she gave her orders knowing that Ted could hardly afford to pay our fares, given his straitened circumstances. I was doubly glad now that I'd paid for our lunch.

I was also glad for the walk. Getting back on a cable car seemed more irritation than adventure, and the day was bright blue and cool. I missed home. On this kind of day, I'd be riding with my father or Joe.

Or Miguel.

I had to force myself to think of that possibility, and again, I felt unease coupled with...guilt. But I pushed those feelings aside, as we talked of Ted's grandfather's case.

Abby questioned Ted about his investigation so far. He'd already done a little digging, he said, by inquiring at some churches in the area, looking for the mysterious Preacher John.

"I've not been able to talk to anyone, yet," he said, his voice raised in chagrin. "Just the housekeepers. The ministers have been out and about."

"You left messages for them?" I asked.

"Yes, but they will hardly be inclined to help me."

"Why not? Your cause is just," I said, indignation coloring my voice.

"It's not that," Abby interjected. "At least, I would hope not. If Ted is leaving cards asking about a Preacher John, and the pastors of the churches haven't heard of him or Ted, they're unlikely to respond. But I'll help."

"How?" Ted asked.

"When we get home, we'll all set to work penning notes to leave at rectories in case the minister is out. We'll include more detail about the mysterious preacher, and we'll suggest they get in touch with me. My mother is well known in churches in the area, as was my father."

"Thank you, Abby. That's most generous of you."

She looked over at me. "You'll help, won't you, Ruth?"

"Why, of course! Give me some note paper, and I'll start writing. Then, perhaps you and I can visit some of the churches together."

Before I knew it, I was swept up in this absorbing task, not realizing until evening fell and Ted had left—he refused Abby's invitation to stay again for dinner as he was intent on getting started on a journey to see his grandfather in San Quentin—that I no longer needed to stay in San Francisco. With Ted's help, my task had been accomplished. I could go home. Just hours earlier, I'd longed for home.

But no more. Now I wanted to stay. And that, I decided, was why a resentful unease had crept into my thoughts of Ted. He—or, at least, his story—was forcing my thoughts away from Miguel.

Chapter Seven

THE NEXT DAY'S VISITS to pastors only added to my restless discomfort, pulling me beyond my grief with the subtlety of a trolley dragging me up a hill while at the same time rocking me between competing loyalties. As much as I respected Ted's mission and felt the need to repay him for his actions on my behalf, I couldn't stop thinking about his grandfather's history with my grandparents. Now that I was finished with my business and free to go home, was it wrong to stay in San Francisco, assisting a man who had hurt my family so long ago? Shouldn't I be more cautious, less trusting?

Whatever my fears or my feelings about the worthiness of Ted's grandfather, I couldn't resist helping Abby, though, who was imbued with zeal, tempered only somewhat by a philosophical outlook. "If he's innocent, our work could help prove it. If not..." She just shrugged. Yes, it was Abby who decided me on whether to stay. I still wanted to get to know her better and to learn about her work.

Ted had left to visit his grandfather the day before, so Abby and I took it upon ourselves to deliver in person the notes we'd penned the day before. Even her mother got in on the plan by writing a few notes of her own to pastors she knew personally through her deceased husband.

It was one of these notes, in fact, that opened the doors at the first church we visited, just a few blocks from the Granville home off of Washington Street. I was relieved that we were walking again this morning, glad to be away from the rattling, raucous cable cars.

We actually found the first pastor in his church, not the rectory, and after Abby introduced herself and me, she handed over the note from her mother which vouched for our good intentions. Then Abby set to explaining the situation with Ted's grandfather, the need to clear him quickly, and the search for the mysterious preacher with the scar on his face.

Before he addressed the latter, he urged us to sit down in a pew near the front of his humble church, a small building with sunshine streaming through tall, unadorned windows. The note in his lap, he stared into space for a moment, a look of peaceful reflection on his pale face. He looked to be beyond seventy with snowy hair and gnarled fingers, and eyes a piercing blue.

"Your father was one of the wisest men I ever met," he said at last to Abby. "No, probably *the* wisest. I miss his companionship and insight into the Lord's word." He patted her hand. "And your mother is a paragon of virtue. She has taught me by her example."

"How so?" Abby whispered, clearly moved by his kind words.

"Well, your father and I used to meet every week to discuss Scripture and various problems we were encountering in our churches. I came to depend on those meetings a great deal, always storing up items I wanted to present to him, knowing he'd make up for my own lack of clarity." He nodded and smiled, sunlight glinting off his face, making him look almost transparent. Only his blue eyes provided a burst of sparkling color.

"When he passed on, I felt quite at sea as week after week passed, and I could not consult him with my troubles. I often found myself waking on our regular meeting day, ready to dash out the door to our usual place—a small park nearby or a coffee shop in colder weather. I sometimes did walk there and sit alone, hoping I'd hear his voice in my ear. Your mother came upon me during one of these outings, and I asked her where she was headed. She was going to the mission to drop off some of your father's clothing. She said it had been hard to think of parting with it, but she knew that he would be disappointed in her if she didn't continue with her charitable work, that he would think she'd only been doing it to please him instead of to help people and to please God.

"Of course, I offered to help her with her task that day, and I learned a valuable lesson. By wallowing in my grief, I had been dishonoring my friend's memory. I had been selfishly cherishing my sadness, turning it from true sorrow into sinful self-pity. I stopped my lonely vigils after that, and I learned to wrestle with my problems without him to guide me, seeking other counsel, praying and figuring things on my own. I'm grateful to your mother for teaching me that lesson."

Her eyes shining, Abby swallowed, then said, "She's a wise woman, too—she and my father were good for each other."

Seeing Abby's melancholy, I rushed to add to the discussion, so she'd have time to compose herself. "You have a lovely church here."

"Why, thank you," he said, beaming. "It's small, but it's a good congregation. I invite you to join us one Sunday."

"Perhaps I will," I said as Abby dabbed at her eyes discreetly. "But in the meantime, do you know of the preacher Abby described to you? Is there such a man in this area?"

He asked for us to describe him again, and Abby had recovered enough to provide the few characteristics we knew. By the end of her recitation, she was her usual spirited self.

"A man's life is at stake," she said, emphasizing the importance of any information he could give us.

He stroked his chin and grimaced. "There are some itinerant preachers who come through now and again. Sometimes they reach out to the established churches, but more often than not, they wander alone. I'm sorry to say that I can't think of one whom I've encountered who fits your description. But I can certainly ask others, and I can provide a list of ministers you might want to talk to." He then led us to his rectory a block away, an extremely modest home with small rooms, neatly tended. While his wife offered hospitality in the form of tea and cookies, he made up his list. We accepted all with gratitude, even though the list contained only a few names not included in our plan.

This visit took a good deal longer than we'd anticipated, so we both sighed as we made our way down the street to the next church.

"This could take forever," Abby said softly. I suspected she was still thinking of the pastor's remarks about her father. I linked my arm in hers for comfort.

"Perhaps we should divide the list and work that way," I suggested.

She smiled at me. "How brave you are—to wander an unknown city on your own! But I can't allow it.

Besides, most of these ministers are ones my father knew personally, so it helps if I am there."

Part of me was relieved she'd not taken me up on my offer. Riding off into an unknown stretch of the valley was invigorating to me. Searching for a mystery man on unknown city streets did fill me with some dread.

"Not every visit will take so much time," I suggested.

"No, of course not," she replied with forced cheer. The brief memory of her father and the observation on the virtue of her mother had shaken her.

This, in turn, shook me. My limited exposure to Abby had shown me a happy, optimistic woman, a determined imp who would make her way in the world on her own terms. But here she was, as unsettled as any grieving daughter, over memories of her deceased father. Yet she'd not shown that side to me at all, and I suspected I wouldn't have seen it yet if the pastor hadn't brought up his own grief.

I'd clung to my grief, though, as if it were a prized possession I must shield from intruders. I'd resented those who'd tried to tear it away from me. I'd worn the raiment of widowhood—even though I'd lost my fiancé, not a husband—for far too long, only abandoning the dark colors for this journey.

What had the pastor said about his own sorrow? He'd realized his sadness had turned into "sinful self-pity." I shivered. Had I not done the same?

"Are you tired? We could stop and have tea somewhere," Abby said, noticing my distress.

"No, no. I'm fine. Let's move along!"

MOVE ALONG WE DID, stopping at church after church, rectory after rectory. My feet ached by the time we were done in the late afternoon, and I welcomed Abby's suggestion to take a cable car back to her neighborhood. We'd hardly made a dent in the list.

"You didn't have to work today?" I asked over the clatter of the machine. Fear no longer bothered me. Fatigue had beat it back.

"I filed my story already for this week. I usually go in to check on various items, though. I might have to stop by tomorrow."

My hand clinging to a pole by our seats, I bit my lip wondering if I dared ask her to take me along. I would love seeing a newspaper office, especially one that hired reportresses. Perhaps after I'd accomplished that goal, I should think of returning home.

Abby placed her gloved hand over mine. "I'll show you the office tomorrow and introduce you around," she said, as if reading my mind. "It will be close to some of the places we've yet to stop by, and I can check my mail while there."

I breathed a relieved sigh. And I smiled. I was enjoying myself, really enjoying myself. I might miss our fresh, open ranch. I might miss my parents and even my brother, but I was having an adventure, getting to know new people who were kind and interesting and engaging in a mission that would have a very real consequence if successful.

WHEN WE FINALLY arrived at the Granville house late in the day, I was surprised to see sitting on a silver tray in the vestibule, a letter addressed to me in my mother's handwriting. I'd only been here a few days, so how could this have reached me so quickly? As I picked it up, Mrs. Granville appeared from the parlor.

"Your traveling companion—Sally Tucker?—dropped this by today. Someone from her family arrived in San Francisco with the note."

My heart pounding, I wanted to rip open the letter and read it immediately. My mother must have rushed to write it and get it in the hands of someone headed my way.

"Abby, why don't you join me in the kitchen?" Mrs. Granville said. "I wanted to ask you about a new recipe."

Grateful for the solitude, I opened the envelope with trembling hands, hoping it contained no bad news about father or Joe or my grandparents.

As soon as I read the first lines, my nerves calmed. There was no bad news from home, only concern about my visit.

"We hope you are safely ensconced at the Granville household and that we will hear from you soon. All is well here, and we eagerly await reports on our friends, your business transactions with the railroad, and, of course, your travel plans for home…."

This was followed by pleasant chatter about ranch goings-on—Joe's successful haggling over a new bull, a fencing section repaired, my grandparents' plans to visit in a week, and then…then the reason for the note became clear, as did my mother's battle with her conscience over whether to send it:

"I am hastening to send you a note because Miguel's sister, Anita, has stopped by on her way to the inland valley. She and her husband are settling there, and we were all too happy to accommodate them on their journey. They have a young babe who is as sweet as he is lively. She asked about you and was disappointed to find you not at home. They will linger for at least a week, perhaps longer."

So that was it. She was letting me know that if I hurried, I could see Anita, a woman whom I'd met only a few times during my courtship because she'd been married and living down the coast at the time. And now it was unlikely I'd ever see her again, if she moved farther into the valley. Mother didn't specifically say that was the reason for her note, of course. I suspected she'd not want me to cut a visit short to resurrect the grief they'd sent me north to escape. But she was being kind enough to alert me to Anita's stay, in case I could come see her.

With a pang of confusion, I folded the letter and climbed the stairs. Yes, I'd love seeing Anita and her little boy—did he look like his deceased uncle, I wondered. Yes, I'd want to talk to her about Miguel, bringing him back to life with our shared memories.

But no, I did not want to go home just yet. I wanted to learn more about Abigail's job and about Ted's quest.

The strange resentment of the day before steamed to my nerve endings, making me on edge and raw. It felt...unfair. Unfair to be torn like this. If I'd stayed on the ranch, I would have enjoyed the visit with Anita with nothing pulling me from its melancholy pleasure.

But wasn't that a sin—to desire that melancholy? Here, I'd started to move beyond it!

Oh, dear, oh, dear—what a muddle my mind was in. I sank onto the bed and stared, as motionless as the air. Just a month ago, I would have been beyond happiness to contemplate seeing Miguel's sister. It would have given me the opportunity to speak of him without fear of my parents' disapproval, to openly share my memories and even my sorrow once again. Now, the thought of that indulgence unsettled me, especially as I remembered the kind pastor we'd spoken with this morning and his words about his own indulgence in self-pity. But maybe facing my temptation was the way to conquer it...I just didn't know anymore.

Should I go home now that my mission was accomplished?

No. I sat up, resolved. I had to help Ted, to repay a debt. He'd helped me, after all, whether I liked it or not. I had to return the favor, whether *I* liked it or not. One luncheon was not sufficient recompense.

Perhaps we'd find what he needed to clear his grandfather, and I could still make it home in time to see my late fiancé's sister. I would write and tell my mother this.

But after I came to this conclusion, I wrestled with how to respond to Mother. She would check the mail daily now, waiting to hear back from me. I had to tell her my business with the railroad was complete—I couldn't lie. And then she'd wonder...why wasn't I returning immediately?

I moved to the desk, pulled out paper and pencil....

My hand poised over the paper, I realized I couldn't answer that question because I myself didn't know the answer. My heart ached, pulling me home and keeping me here.

Finally, I wrote thanking her for the news of Anita and promising to let her know when I could return.

"Please give Anita and her family my deepest affection," I wrote. "But don't have her linger on my account if they feel they must go. Although I dearly want to see them, my business isn't quite finished here yet. Your loving daughter, Ruth."

That wasn't a lie. My business wasn't finished here yet—my business in repaying Ted's favor by helping him.

As I sat at the small desk by the window, the thought of Ted pinched my heart. Yes, he could be infuriating, and his ability to slip so easily into a charade bothered me, but…he intrigued me. I wanted to know more about him. The way he'd gathered information from me on the trolley ride in order to make a stronger case to the railroad agent—that was brilliant. And it had been kind, as well, as he'd attempted to distract me from my fears on the cable car. I'd also admired how he'd finally made my father's case—when he'd finally gotten around to it, of course. He'd been direct and sincere, and sharply focused. He had a good mind, that was sure.

Had Miguel? The thought made me grimace. The idea that I'd even thought to pose that question to myself saddened me.

What had we talked about? The ranch mostly. And what he wanted to do with the property he would buy for us. How to get the most from the land.

Yes, he was smart. But in a different way, on different topics.

I stretched, tired both physically and emotionally.

A gentle knock roused me from my dilemma. Abby asked if she could enter.

"Come on in," I said, turning toward the door. When she stepped in the room, I immediately grinned. A smudge of flour dusted her skirt and nose. When I pointed it out, she just shook her head and laughed.

"I'm a lost cause. I trust you'll help me tidy up." When she sat on the edge of the bed, I did just that, moistening a handkerchief and patting away the offending bits of flour.

"I don't mean to pry," she said after the cleansing act was over, "but I thought I should ask if everything is all right at home. You received a letter, I couldn't help noticing."

I nodded and told her about its contents.

She commiserated. "Mother told me about your fiancé," she said. "I know it must still pain you terribly. But I'd hate to see you leave now!" she exclaimed. "You've been such a wonderful companion. And I think Ted likes having you along, as well."

"I—I have liked it, too—helping out, that is. But I shouldn't impose on your hospitality. My task is completed, after all. I only feel an obligation to Ted and..." I looked down at the letter in my hands. Returning to the ranch now would seem lonely.

"And you are torn," Abby said, reaching for my hands. "Of course you are! Your fiancé's sister! You must feel awful about not rushing to see her. I'm being selfish wanting you to stay."

"I do want to help Ted," I offered, now feeling that she might be pushing me toward leaving. "I don't feel right about abandoning his cause even though..."

"Even though his grandfather hurt our families?" When I nodded, she continued: "I think this bothers Mother, too, but I believe the truth will out, and if the man is innocent, and we had a chance to help but didn't...." She smiled softly. "As to Ted, you wouldn't be 'abandoning' him if you decided you should go," she said. "But I know he values your help." She stared into my eyes then, with that frank brightness I was already beginning to cherish and depend on. "Ruth, we'll see how we do with Ted's grandfather's case in the next few days. Perhaps you can put off making a decision about returning until we gather some more information."

I nodded, not telling her I'd come to this conclusion on my own already.

She patted my hand. "And then, if you decide to leave, we shall plan visits with each other."

"Yes! I had been thinking that very thing," I said, looking up.

"Of course I'll visit you!" she said, hurrying to stand and put her arm around my shoulder. "But I mean it when I say you've been a good companion. You've been more than that. You've been a help, and this is important business we're engaged in. A man's life is at stake."

Yes, a man's life. That was more important than any desire to see Anita, surely. If the man were truly innocent.

Abby twisted her mouth to one side and spoke again, this time taking the subject into a different direction. "I've been thinking, Ruth. Billy Crane should make amends. If he's truly remorseful for his past and has changed his ways, he should offer atonement."

"What do you mean?"

"He should ask for your grandparents' forgiveness."

My hand fluttered to my chest at the thought of putting this man, who'd clearly wronged my grandparents so many years ago, back in touch with them. If he had tried to kill them, they'd be rightfully offended and hurt if I shared their whereabouts with him, even if he were confined.

"I can't possibly allow that—him to contact them, that is."

Abby nodded in understanding.

"Ted will probably tell him he's working with you. Ted could ask him if he'd like to say anything to your grandparents…through you."

Me—what a responsibility! I let out a quick breath. My parents and grandparents were gentle, virtuous souls. They understood that people could change, that they could redeem themselves. But this was asking a great deal of them, even to consider an apology. I thought again of Miguel. Although he'd been a good man, I knew there were some who'd disliked him. A rancher near our homestead, in particular, had not wanted to deal with him because he'd considered Miguel too "uppity." For that reason, my beloved had traveled below the Big Sur to make a deal on horses two years ago. I'd always felt a rush of animosity when seeing this rancher since Miguel's death, wondering if tragedy could have been avoided had the rancher sold horses to Miguel. If that man had contacted my family, offering his remorse for his poor treatment of Miguel, would I have been open to his words? Or would I be horrified to think my parents had allowed him into my life?

But my parents were better people than I was, were they not? My grandparents were the best of humankind. Surely, if Billy Crane's apology were sincere, they could find it in their hearts, if not to forgive the man, at least to lay aside any objections they'd have with me working with his grandson to spare his life. I had to tell them that eventually, after all.

"Is sending a telegram very expensive?" I asked.

"Not unreasonably so," Abby answered.

"I think I need to let my parents know right away that I won't be coming home soon," I said, determination building in my heart. The letter would be insufficient. "I need to reassure them, too." Maybe then I could reassure myself.

WE HAD VERY little time before dinner, but Abby helped me write a telegram to my parents letting them know that I was well and safe, happy to hear of Anita's visit, and that I'd be writing them shortly about my plans to stay in San Francisco. The message ended with "please do not worry."

Abby gave the note to a servant, a boy who tended their horses in a nearby livery stable, just as we heard her mother call us to the dining room.

As I turned the corner into the lovely room, I was surprised to see Ted sitting at the table. My spirits rose so quickly that it startled me. I hadn't realized how much I'd looked forward to seeing him again.

"I invited Mr. Beaumont to dine with us," Mrs. Granville said when he rose from his seat as we made our way to the table. "I sent word round to his boarding house."

"What a pleasant surprise! I didn't think we'd see you until tomorrow," Abby exclaimed.

"It was equally pleasant to receive your mother's invitation. I received it just as I arrived back in the city," Ted said, then looked at me with a shy smile. "I was hoping you would still be in town, too, Ruth. When do you have to go home?"

Despite myself, I felt a blush warming my cheeks. I looked down, happy that Abby decided to answer for me.

"She's not yet made her travel arrangements, Ted. She's going to stay a bit longer to help us out with your father's case and to visit with us." She then went on to report the bad news of our fruitless search for the mystery minister that day.

Ted frowned. "How many more are there to visit?" he asked somberly.

"Oh, quite a few," I offered, trying to comfort him and assure myself. If there was the possibility that an alibi were still out there, his grandfather was indeed innocent. "I mean, enough to keep us busy tomorrow and possibly the next day. I'm sure we'll encounter someone who knows this preacher."

"I appreciate your optimism, Ruth, but time is running short, and my grandfather is not a strong man." He looked down at his soup as if he had no appetite. "When I visited with him today, he appeared to be ill. The prison is damp and drafty. And, of course, they offer little in the way of medical attention, given his impending…circumstances."

"Oh, dear," Mrs. Granville murmured. "We shall have to say a prayer for him." She proceeded to add Billy Crane to the grace she led us in. Then we all began to eat, even Ted, who, despite his mood, now seemed hungry. He must have been frugally watching his money, I imagined, which made me even gladder that I'd paid for our lunches yesterday.

"Were you able to get any more information from your grandfather, anything that could help?" I asked.

"A few more details, but not much, I'm afraid." He finished his soup and tore off a piece of bread. "He thinks he knows the gang responsible for the crime. He suspects they've hidden their take and won't spend it until after his hanging—" He stopped and looked down. "—I'm sorry. I shouldn't be mentioning such rough material here."

"Nonsense. It's the truth. Honesty is nothing to be ashamed of, nor to cover up," Abby said.

"Go on, Ted," Mrs. Granville prodded. "Your grandfather believes the gang responsible isn't using their riches? Why not? He's been charged and tried as responsible."

"He said one of their group years ago got into a spending spree after a bank robbery, thinking he was safe when another man had been charged with the crime. Then, that fellow ended up being cleared and the real villain was fingered and couldn't account for where he'd gotten all his money. Now they don't take chances, my grandfather says."

So they would wait until Billy Crane was dead before using their loot.

"I'm surprised they'd have the patience for such a plot," I said. "One would expect men who choose to rob rather than work for a living to be reckless."

"Yes," Ted mused. "But grandfather pointed out to me they had gotten much better over the years at planning their thievery, putting as much effort into it as they would into a day's honest labor. He said it became a matter of habit for some of them, their way of life, that they feasted on the excitement as much as the reward, sad to say."

"He knew these men well?" I asked, beginning to grow uneasy. Billy Crane's conversion had been recent and could be shallow.

"Unfortunately, yes," Ted said, serving himself some lamb stew. "He's not proud of those acquaintances, but I'm hoping his knowledge of their modus operandi could help save him."

"If the stolen goods are found, and it's clear who hid them, that would save him, wouldn't it?" Abby asked. "Exactly what was stolen again?"

"Gold, of course," said Ted between mouthfuls. The poor lad did seem awfully hungry. Had he eaten at all today? "But also a watch and a ring, according to the sheriff's reports from the now deceased 'witness.' If we were to find them, it's possible we could trace them back to the real thieves and murderers."

I thought about this as I ate. Finally, I asked, "Does your grandfather know of their usual hideaways?"

"He's provided me with a list of those he knows. But he'd forsaken that life, even before he'd completely repented of his ways. So his knowledge is limited. And they surely would have changed their secret places over time."

"You never know," said Abby excitedly. "If they're prideful, they might assume no one would be on to their wily ways. We should investigate!"

Ted shook his head slowly. "I am afraid I could not allow that. Looking into their hiding places might be risky business, and I would not place you in jeopardy."

Mrs. Granville nodded. "I'm happy to hear you say that. It speaks well of you." She looked at Abby. "Adventures are fine, my dear, when undertaken with appropriate caution. Mr. Crane here understands the dangers involved and will prepare accordingly. You would probably hinder his ability more than help him with his quest in these circumstances."

I wanted to say that I would be more than willing to help, taking the appropriate cautions, but I was afraid of encouraging Abby's proclivity to embrace the unknown. I didn't want to put her crosswise with her mother, any more than she already was with her.

Speaking of that amiable tension, they soon commenced their usual subtle bickering, with Mrs. Granville asking Abby if she'd worn that same skirt to her appointments when she had a fine new suit she could have put on instead. This led to Abby complaining about finery that was soon "ink-stained and ruined" at the newspaper, which then led to Mrs. Granville suggesting that perhaps newspaper work wasn't the best choice for a woman.

From there—well, it ranged from the deeper issue of women's place in the world to a less consequential debate over whether strawberries would be out early this year. There seemed to be no topic upon which they couldn't find a source of disagreement. It seemed, at times, as if this were a great puzzle they enjoyed laboring over.

Ted and I often exchanged smiling wide-eyed glances during this chatter. To both of us, I dare say, it was akin to watching a theatrical performance filled with melodrama one moment and farcical comedy the next.

After a pound cake was served with coffee, we all went to retire to the parlor, where Mrs. Granville tried to persuade Abby to play the piano for us while she protested she'd not touched the instrument in months. This set up another round of battle between mother and daughter, but it was just the diversion I needed to address with Ted the topic Abby and I had discussed earlier.

While Abby fussed about what music to play, and Mrs. Granville made suggestions that her daughter summarily rejected, I spoke quietly with Ted.

"I was wondering if you mentioned to your grandfather that you have encountered me, the granddaughter of Kate and Daniel Winchester, here. Do you know of the relationship?"

He grimaced slightly before nodding. "Yes, I do. He spoke of it today when I mentioned the help I was receiving from you and Abby. I explained who you were, your families, and he didn't hesitate to tell the awful tale," he said, looking uncomfortable, a crease scarring his brow. "It was not a happy subject, and I apologize for bringing you into this case when your family had been hurt by his previous malfeasance. When I first met you, I did not know the full story, only that he'd been on a wagon train with a Daniel Winchester as trail guide—that much he'd shared. The Granvilles made me aware of the rest of the story my first evening here, of course, but not all the details. My grandfather confessed to them, and I almost wished he hadn't."

"What was his reaction, if I may ask, when you told him of meeting me?"

"It pained him," Ted continued softly. "He remembered them very clearly. He said he'd thought of them often over the years and hoped they were happy. When I told him they were still alive, it lifted his spirits considerably. He said it was one of the greatest regrets of his life how badly he'd acted back then. His bad deeds after that were always in pursuit of fortune. His treatment of them was sheer meanness, he said, borne of envy and grief over his brother's passing during the trail ride west."

This calmed me, but still, I couldn't help wondering if the man's words were sincere. How could one tell? If only I could have seen with my own eyes…

"Ted, do you think—" I didn't know how to put it, how to ask if his grandfather was truly remorseful. What right did I have to ask that, of a man facing certain death? That prospect alone was enough to scour a man's soul of ill will, wasn't it? Why did I have to "hear" his regret, see it? And even if I did, how sincere an effort would it be if someone *suggested* he ask for forgiveness? Shouldn't it spring spontaneously from his own heart?

"I know," Ted said, impulsively putting his hand over mine. "I know what you must be thinking. Now that he knows your grandparents are still alive, he should ask for their forgiveness. I…I didn't think it right to suggest this." He looked down.

I breathed a sigh of relief. Ted understood. He knew one couldn't prompt such a thing, that it had to be his grandfather's initiative. "Of course you couldn't!" I quickly assured him. "I was just wondering if he would come to that conclusion on his own."

"I wouldn't be surprised if he did," Ted said. "I've only gotten to know my grandfather through these few encounters, but he seems truly remorseful."

"Your mother never spoke of him?" I prodded. "He's her father."

He shook his head. "She was raised by her mother without him around—just as my sister and I grew up without our father. She knew from her mother he was not fit for society, that she'd rued the day she'd married him, and that she'd be better off keeping the union as quiet as possible so that her daughter—my mother—could make a good match."

"What an awful burden those memories must have been for your mother and grandmother. Is she still alive?"

"Oh, no. Long since gone. My mother says she was a spirited and intelligent woman, and that her rebelliousness was what led to her marriage to grandfather. She'd traveled west, my grandmother, for adventure. Apparently, she found it, staying with a local pastor and his family, tending children in a small orphanage. Then she met my grandfather and he managed to charm her, I was told, and she thought she'd converted him to a better life. It lasted but a year until he was thrown in jail for some misdemeanor, one of many incarcerations. By that time, she had a child—my mother—to tend to, so she returned East."

"Does he speak of her?"

"Only once. He told me he wished he could tell her how sorry he was." He leaned toward me. "Now he can say he is sorry, though, to people still living. I'm sure he'll write something to your parents and grandparents, Ruth."

My earlier fears suddenly returned. "But he can't write to them at the ranch!" I exclaimed. "I'm sure they'd feel that he was somehow—"

"Standing at their doorstep? That would definitely be an upsetting renewal of an acquaintance that I have no doubt they'd like to forget. I don't mean to disparage your grandparents' openness to the atoning sinner, but it is only natural they would be wary."

Relieved that Ted saw the situation exactly as I did, I put forward my idea. "If he were to ask for forgiveness, or to offer his apology for what he'd done to them, I suggest he do it through an intermediary. I could make sure they received whatever message he decided to write."

At that news, Ted smiled and squeezed my hand, sending a flutter up to my cheeks, flushing them with warmth again. "You're a good person, Ruth. But I don't know if I'd want to place you in that position. Let me think about it…"

"You misjudge me," I hastened to add. "I'm not as good a person as you think. I just want to protect my grandparents should the note—if he writes one—be…be something…troubling."

He continued to smile.

"Thank you so much, Ruth. I know this puts you in a difficult position. I promise not to abuse your good nature. If my grandfather does want to make amends, I will make sure that the message goes through you. And I object to your judgment of yourself. You are as good a person as I think. Possibly even better."

Once again he squeezed my hand. Once again, I caught my breath, and my thoughts became muddled. Fortunately, at that moment, Abby had finished her squabbling and actually began playing something, a beautiful, if somewhat melancholy piece, made less so by her occasional soft outbursts whenever she hit a wrong note.

At the end of the piece, Ted retracted his hand from mine to applaud, and I immediately felt his absence. I looked into his eyes as we both clapped and thought I saw something there—regret, longing, anticipation? I didn't know if it was the music or his grandfather's sad story or just the sweet spring twilight with its promise of beautiful mild mornings to come, but I felt intoxicated with a peaceful joy, something I'd not felt since Miguel's death.

Chapter Eight

THAT NIGHT, BEFORE going to bed, I wrote yet another letter to my mother, a painful letter because I knew she'd worry when she read it. I crumpled my earlier one, now that I'd sent the reassuring telegram, and I instead wrote from my heart, telling her how much I wanted to see Anita but that I also wanted to help Ted. And I poured out his story and that of his grandfather, letting her know I knew he'd caused the family pain in the past.

It was odd to think how careless I'd been with Mother's feelings at home, at all the times I'd railed against her efforts to pull me from grief to the wider world. Now, miles away, I could see how much she loved me and how much I hurt her when we disagreed or I was intransigent.

In my note, I assured her that Ted's grandfather, Billy Crane, was imprisoned and of no danger to anyone. But I also told her of his sentence and Ted's efforts to free him. "He is a reformed man, Ted assures us, and I trust him." Yes, I trusted Ted. But his grandfather? How awful it must have been to hear him talk of how he'd abandoned Ted's grandmother, with a small babe to raise. And Ted himself had experienced a fatherless home since his own father was deceased. Whatever my sadness, it didn't equal those events.

I sat at the little desk in the glow of moonlight after I'd finished my letter. How was Ted living? Mrs. Granville had said a boarding house. From the way he'd polished off his dinner, he clearly didn't have a lot of money to spare. Whatever acclaim he received from proving his grandfather's innocence would not result in immediate recompense. It would still take time to turn the reputation he would earn into money. He'd said he had a sister to support. I could only assume she was being taken care of in some way for the time being, or he wouldn't have left her back in New York.

The poor fellow—so much responsibility, with the clock ticking on his current task.

I stood and stretched, stiff from a day largely spent sitting in various rectory parlors. How I longed to be riding!

My eyes widened. Then riding I would do. In the morning, I would insist Abby handle the church calls and we would put off the newspaper office visit for another day. As for me—I would go with Ted to seek the gang members' hideaways. Yes, he would protest. Yes, Mrs. Granville would object. But I was confident my stubborn will would defeat them all.

IN THE MORNING, I was in such a frenetic state that I'd ignited a headache. My temples throbbed so that I could truthfully tell Abby my poor skull needed a rest. She and her mother both hovered over me like Florence Nightingales-in-training, fetching a special Chinese tea and urging me to lie about all day while they went on with their work—Mrs. Granville to her charity chores and Abby to visiting more churches on Billy Crane's behalf since I'd be unable to join her for the newspaper visit, and she needn't appear there anyway. I inquired about their horses and if I could ride one, knowing the out-of-doors would do wonders for my head. Here, too, was no lie. Even as I asked them, my pulse raced at the thought of sitting in a saddle.

Although they were full of admonitions and advice about riding too far or going into unseemly areas, they agreed that I would probably benefit from a return to my ranch routine, which they knew had included daily rides. They made the necessary arrangements with their stable boy.

As soon as they left, the hush of the house whispered my aches away as if blowing from my head a burden I'd not known was there. The Granvilles were enormously lovable but also a presence—the two of them together—never to be ignored.

I'd not made a specific plan to meet Ted today, but I set about finding him as quickly as I was able. I asked the housekeeper how to get a message to him, and she arranged for the stable boy to take a note to him at his boardinghouse, the address of which she had from a message Abigail had sent to him about coming to dinner again. My note merely said I needed his help and would he stop by, bringing riding clothes if possible. I also had the servant post my letter home.

Nervously, I changed into riding clothes that I'd brought with me, not knowing if they'd be of use. Like most of the rest of my travel wardrobe, they were new, and I smiled and said a silent thanksgiving for my mother's own stubbornness in insisting I be reasonably outfitted. Now I turned in front of the cheval mirror, admiring how my split skirt, of a dark green suede, suited my coloring and my figure.

But more than how it made me look was how it made me feel. With my old riding boots—these I'd refused to replace—the clothes made me feel more like myself again, the Ruth from my father's ranch who would ride almost all day and never mind, who loved horses and their gentle alertness to the wider world.

With an eagerness I'd not felt in a long time, I rushed downstairs when I heard the door bell clang, beating the housekeeper to the task of opening it.

Ted stood there, his face rosy from effort and a fine line of perspiration on his brow at the hairline, his hat held before him with both hands.

"Is everything all right?" he asked immediately, his eyes searching mine for signs of distress.

"Yes, yes," I said, now feeling embarrassed by the brevity of my note, which had obviously seemed a call for emergency aid of some kind. "Come in, please," I said, looking down, too shamed to face his gaze. "I didn't mean to alarm you. I'm sorry."

After stepping into the foyer, he reached out and gently touched my arm. "No need for apologies. I'm just relieved you're all right."

"I'm afraid I was too cryptic," I said, leading him into the parlor, now feeling even more embarrassed. What had I been thinking when I'd concocted this plan? I shook my head just a little, as if that would bring my usual straightforward common sense back to the fore.

After urging him to sit—he looked as if he'd ran all the way from his boardinghouse here and was still slightly breathless from the effort—I rested on the edge of the chair opposite him.

"I—I awakened with a head full of cobwebs," I began. "A good ride will clear them, and I was hoping a man's company would keep my hostesses from worrying too much on my behalf."

A small smile tugged at the corner of his mouth, and his gaze pierced me. "I see," he said. I noticed that he wasn't wearing his usual suit but rather denim trousers and rough corduroy jacket, as well as what appeared to be much-used boots. The hat he held, too, was different than his usual cap. This one was more of the western style, the kind my father wore, with a wide brim and string clasp.

When he didn't say more, I continued, now feeling a dreadful need to fill any silence with talk—explanations, excuses, ramblings that would lead me out of the thicket into which I'd driven my pride.

"And," I said with the same steel will I'd often used on my parents, "I hope to help you in your investigation of the many hideaways thieves might use to stow their fortunes." Head held high, I stared at him…down my nose.

At this, he laughed. No, I'd say a more accurate description would be a guffaw, a full-throated chuckle emanating from deep within. He bent over with humor, in fact, his hat shaking between his knees with the rigor of his amusement.

Without thinking, I pursed my lips and inwardly raged. I had been prepared to battle him on my inclusion in his expedition. I had not been prepared to be laughed at.

"I hadn't realized you'd procured a drink before heading here. I thought you said you weren't a drinking man. I need no chaperone to ride, so you need not stay. Thank you so much for coming by," I said, standing.

"A drink? Wha—" His laughter halted swiftly as his face colored with irritation. "You accuse me of imbibing—and at this hour?"

"It's the only reason I can think of for your sudden hilarity. I can't imagine what else would have caused such a laughing fit." I stared at him as if to dare him. "Surely a gentleman doesn't laugh at a lady like that."

He stood, too, grabbing his hat so firmly he was crushing its rim. "Now, Ruth, don't get all uppity about a little harmless…"

"Mockery. I think that's what it was. Mockery."

"No, more like surprise. That you would be so fearless. But, of course, I should have imagined all women in this household to be of that nature. It seems to infect you here."

"Was that compliment or insult?" I said thinly.

"Since when is honesty either?"

Honesty—that was Abigail's theme. Honesty is no insult, she would have said. As the memory teased at my mind, my mood softened. Perhaps sensing my shift in temperament, he spoke more softly.

"I would not want to place you in danger. I can't possibly take you with me today. And, besides, we'd have no chaperone, something I'm sure Mrs. Granville would want, and, I, too, would recommend, since it's not smiled upon for a young man to accompany a young woman unchaperoned…."

"Then I shall go alone. I'll ask the stable boy what routes to pursue. I'm sure he can provide direction to a suitable guide."

"And then what? You take off on your own? It can be dangerous. It's not just who you might run into but what. Snakes, for example."

"Ah, that's so true. We never see snakes in Carmel Valley. What exactly do they look like?"

"Now you mock *me*," he said in a wounded tone.

"Honesty is no…" I stopped, realizing I was about to imitate Abigail. At this point, a smile began to spread on his face, no doubt triggered by our mutual thoughts of dauntless Abby. We both laughed then, slow gentle giggles that shook our shoulders and brought tears of joy to my eyes.

My eyes—Ted looked into them. Stared so deeply that I almost felt compelled to look away. His stare left me breathless. It was as if he were seeing something of my soul laid bare. It sent a shiver through me, a tremble magnified when he impulsively grabbed my arms and kissed me! Gentle and sweet and, oh, so, so welcome. I'd not realized how much I'd yearned for such a kiss, how much I'd missed being liked in that way by a man.

When he pulled away, his face registered shock. "Do excuse me, Ruth. I take liberties, terrible liberties," he said self-consciously straightening at the sound of the housekeeper in the kitchen.

"No need for apologies," I whispered, still stirred by the intimacy. "You could not take what I wasn't willing to give."

For an awkward few seconds we stood facing each other until he cleared his throat and suggested we get going.

"Ordinarily, I would not presume to accompany a young lady without a suitable chaperone," he said gruffly, "but since you are determined to go alone if I don't agree, then we shall set out together. I would ask that you assure Mrs. Granville that I did not lure you into the hills with base intent. I will be a perfect gentleman, I assure you."

The question of whether I would go with him seemed to have been settled.

THAT DAY I FELT I'd rediscovered myself. We rode into the hills around the city, and Ted was a strong and confident guide. I'd not taken him for a man to be so comfortable on a horse, but he told me that equestrian work had been part of his studies in New York and that he'd even won several ribbons as a boy in both dressage and jumping.

In fact, I'd originally intended to take the feistier of the steeds we used that day, figuring I would be able to handle him with my background on the ranch. But Ted immediately established a rapport with the massive beast and rode him with such strength and sureness that the horse seemed docile under his hands.

We might have been searching for hideaways and secret places, but we spent the day either riding strong and hard or ambling while we talked, both companionable exercises that left us content and happy. If not for the dire circumstances propelling our search, one would have thought we were picnicking courters out for a day's ride.

When Ted became thoughtful to the point of brooding, I asked him about his grandfather.

"You must be terribly worried. How much time is there?" I asked, knowing it was a blunt question but hoping he wouldn't be hurt by it.

"A month, maybe more. I've asked for delays and have been granted one. I have a few legal tricks up my sleeve to keep them going."

"But eventually the fuse will burn out." Our horses picked carefully over broken rocks at the top of a hill while we sat at the crest and stared at a crystal blue sky over the shimmering harbor. San Francisco's rooftops gleamed in the sun, and I could see a cable car being inexorably pulled to the top of a hill's peak. From this distance, it looked so calm and easy, like a child's toy.

The wind blew my hair and ruffled my neck scarf. I breathed deeply. This was the air of the ranch, peaceful and powerful.

"That it will."

"Ted," I said slowly, "have you prepared yourself...for the worst?"

His brow furrowed, he stared hard at me and swallowed before answering. "The worst could be many things." He looked down.

"What do you mean?"

"I want to believe...." He trailed off and looked away.

It took me a moment, but I figured out his meaning. He was afraid his grandfather might really be guilty. So, he wasn't blindly loyal to his blood kin. He, too, wondered if his grandfather's conversion was real. Poor man! What a burden to carry! It made sympathy well in my chest, and admiration, as well. I was relieved to know that he didn't just accept unquestioningly his grandfather's innocence based on their family ties, but, rather, was beset by the normal doubts of a rational mind.

Biting my lower lip, I impulsively leaned over and placed my gloved hand over his. "Ted, you have no choice but to believe. Without faith, how could you serve him well? And he is your grandfather."

He looked me in the eyes, a small smile playing at his lips. "Precisely. I tell myself—well, I know this will reflect on me poorly—but the people who were killed were robbers and killers themselves. So I tell myself that even if Grandfather did do the deed..."

"He rid the world of dangerous men," I finished. Again, my heart went out to him—to carry such a burden must have been exhausting, a constant struggle to push against the weight. And yet he'd given no impression of wrestling with this grave challenge. "You must continue to tell yourself that if you are to acquit him. And perhaps you can attempt to keep him on the right path."

"Even so—if he did do it—he took the law into his own hands. And he might not have known—if he did it—their guilty state before…"

He stopped and looked into the distance. The poor man—in his heart he wrestled hourly with his grandfather's possible guilt, yet he forced himself to plod forward, just as we'd urged our horses to keep up the hill, carrying their heavy loads just as he hefted his own internal burden.

"I understand," I whispered. "It was wrong, regardless of the sins perpetrated by the victims. Your grand…the criminal had no right to their lives or their goods, no matter how ill-gotten they were."

"Yes," he said sadly.

"But, Ted, you must believe him. It is all you can do. You must assume he is telling you—his own flesh-and-blood—the truth. You have no choice." The bonds of family, even those strained by absence and wrongdoing, were strong. I would have defended my kin with the same vigor, even in the face of hard evidence to the contrary, until there was no other choice but to disbelieve.

"That is the way I feel." He looked at me, relief and gratitude in his soft eyes.

"If it will set your mind at ease," I suggested, "perhaps you could have someone talk to your grandfather, about…about setting his soul to rights…."

"I've asked a minister to visit him. He says he appreciates that."

"And is this—this search for the real thieves' hideaway—the best hope?" I asked, starting to feel guilty we were dawdling and that I might be keeping him from his task.

"It's the best I can think of, outside of some legal issues I've dealt with already and the search for the preacher. I'm stalling things for now, but that will cease eventually."

I took a deep breath. Despite our heavy conversation, I was enjoying this time outside.

"Come on, then. Let's keep exploring," I said, giving my horse a little shake on the reins. We stepped forward.

Ted smiled and did the same. "You seem so at home out here."

"I come from a ranch, remember," I said. "My happiest moments were riding hard with …with a man named Miguel. We'd race each other. I often beat him. Or maybe…he *let* me beat him." The feel of the wind on my face, of being one with the horse, of laughing as Miguel looked over at me—it took my breath away.

"Mrs. Granville told me about your loss. You miss Miguel terribly," Ted said simply, with no rancor, only understanding.

"Yes, I do." We let our horses amble, Ted's gaze flicking to various spots as he looked for familiar territory. "But I shouldn't let it taint our day. I should be able to let go. It's been a long time now. Two years."

"Is that what everyone tells you?"

"Yes."

"But you resent it."

I nodded. "I'm afraid so. I'm sure my parents concocted this trip to get me to let go. But it seems so…traitorous to me. I mean, Miguel was my fiancé. We were going to spend our lives together. I can't just throw him on a trash pile, his memory to be burned up and gone with the smoke." As I spoke, my voice trembled. I felt tears well in my eyes and forcefully shook them off. Why was I telling Ted these things?

After a sympathetic glance, he did not talk for a few moments as he continued to scour the countryside for the hideaways he sought. I saw his gaze linger on a spot in the hills where I thought I spotted a flash of light. "What was that?" I asked.

"Nothing," he said quickly. Too quickly—I was beginning to wonder if he, too, felt I should just "move on" but was too polite to say it outright. Finally, after ten minutes of wandering, his gaze flicking back to the spot I'd seen the flash, he stopped and looked at me.

"I think we should be getting back. I'll have to talk to Grandfather again about his memories of lairs."

As we tread carefully down steep inclines, he remained focused on the journey, keeping in front of me to gallantly check the path before I came down. At a narrow plateau, he picked up the thread of conversation about my grief, as if we'd not dropped the earlier topic.

"When I am overcome with memories of my losses, I struggle to remind myself of what I have left and what I have yet to gain." His eyes, narrowed against the sun even under the brim of his hat, seemed to glint with meaning.

I reddened as I contemplated his own losses—his parents and his fortune, such as it had been. A life he'd lived, whereas my loss was but a life I'd hoped to live— that as wife to Miguel. My cheeks warm with shame, I looked down. My hands clutched the reins tightly. Twice since coming to San Francisco—once with the pastor grieving Abby's father's death and now with Ted—I was being reminded that my own sorrow had an element of self-pity to it. I wanted to shake it off. I truly did. But it sometimes wrapped itself around me, like a sheet sprung free by wind from a line of laundry. Was this what temptation was—not grabbing all the glittering things that held no appeal for me but embracing rather than pushing away the one thing that made me feel special?

"I am not diminishing your grief, Ruth. No one can or should take it away from you. It's a reminder of a good part of your life. I only mean to console."

I nodded, unable to speak. He was right, of course. And, unlike others' similar attempts to gently nudge me beyond my sadness, his words both warmed and rebuked me, but in the tenderest of ways.

"It's sinful for me to dwell on those memories," I said at last.

Quickly, he turned to me. "Don't think that, Ruth. You just need to learn how to remember him without losing yourself and your future in the memories."

"Is that what you do? I mean, your own loss, of your mother and of your father years ago—they don't seem to have colored your outlook on life."

He smiled ruefully. "I struggle, as we all do, to reconcile the dark with the light in life. I try to remind myself that it's all part of a greater whole, and to focus on my blessings."

"You seem to be good at that," I said, admiring him. "I shall have to learn from you."

His face reddened at the compliment, and he turned away.

"Look there," he said, pointing to a flat stretch that led into town after our next hill was descended. "I'll race you to the train crossing once we reach the valley."

With a soft cluck of his tongue, we moved on. And when our horses' hooves touched flat earth a few moments later, he but glanced at me with a smile, and we both kicked our heels at the same time, lowering our bodies to the manes of our steeds.

Wind blew my hat down my back and blossomed the sleeves of my light jacket. Earth sprang up under the animals' great strides, muddying my gloves and peppering my face. But I didn't care! I laughed. And so, it seemed to me, did the horses. After being so careful with their footing on the hills, they seemed just as eager as we were to let go and sprint forward, their strong muscles stretching as they pounded the ground to push us forward.

By the time we reached the train crossing into town, both Ted and I were laughing out loud, our voices a song of praise for the glorious day, sun warming our shoulders and fresh air filling our lungs.

"You are the victor," I said, pretending to pout.

Ted grinned, ear to ear. "That's right. You'll never need to worry about me just letting you win, Ruth. Whatever you accomplish will be done fair and square."

That brought an answering smile from me. No, he was not Miguel. He was his own person. And I liked him.

Chapter Nine

BACK AT THE Granville house, I was able to sneak in and wash up before Abigail or her mother came back, and Ted felt too disheveled to join us for dinner, despite my invitation. I was taking a liberty inviting him, but I had no doubt the Granvilles would have asked him had they been around at the time of our arrival. He didn't linger, standing chivalrously on the doorsill, not coming in, knowing only the housekeeper was at home. He'd not sully my reputation, he said, by staying in the house with me unchaperoned, despite our ride in that state.

I half expected him to kiss me—no, I fully expected it—but he held back, nervously toying with the brim of his hat while he wished me a good evening. If anything, he seemed a little eager to be on his way, making me wonder if he planned to revisit the hills, investigating the area he'd scrutinized from afar.

I felt curiously on edge, excited, as I washed and dressed in clean clothes, thinking first of the deepening friendship with Ted and second of his distraction as he'd gazed into the distance.

He'd seen something there, I realized. And he'd skillfully maneuvered me away from it, even suggesting the race at the end of our excursion—had he wanted me out of the area quickly?

Now my excitement turned a bit into worry, so by the time I joined Abigail and her mother for dinner after they'd returned, I was a bit out of sorts, something that Abby noticed before the first course was cleared. In response to her inquiry about my mood, I told her my theory about Ted and the flash of light in the distance after sheepishly confessing to going riding with him that day.

"He must have found something!" Abby exclaimed, her hands carelessly brushing a fork from the table. While her mother tsk-ed, Abby bent over and retrieved it, breathing on its surface and rubbing it with a bit of her skirt. I thought I heard her mother groan. "Maybe the hideaway of the gang his grandfather thinks did the deed?"

"I'm sure he was going back to investigate on his own," I offered.

"Oh, dear," Mrs. Granville said. "Should we notify authorities?"

"I don't see the San Francisco police scrabbling up in those hills on a wild-goose chase," Abby responded.

"We shouldn't jump to the conclusion that they won't," Mrs. Granville said.

"We should, however, jump to the conclusion that the city government is so corrupt that President Roosevelt has been petitioned to address it. I sometimes wonder if the police department is any better."

"Abby! We shouldn't cast aspersions on those who have not offended us or whose offenses are unproven!"

And so they went for a good quarter hour as the housekeeper served a roast. I felt, once again, like a spectator viewing a play, my head bobbing from one to the other as they each tried to prove their points, the flow of their thoughts only occasionally interrupted by a remonstrance from Mrs. Granville for Abby to "straighten those loose locks," or "wash out that spot before wearing that blouse again." At the end of their debate, Abby looked at me curiously, as if trying to remember what I'd said that had begun their adversarial romp through local politics.

"I'm sure Ted will be fine. He won't take any unnecessary chances," she said to console me, "knowing his grandfather is so dependent on him."

"His lifeline, really," Mrs. Granville agreed.

Looking at my nearly untouched plate, Abby's eyes sparkled. "But I will be sure to tell him your appetite fled at the thought of him being in jeopardy."

I blushed, feeling the warm blood redden my cheeks.

Abby snorted out a laugh. "No need to be embarrassed, Ruth. He's a very charming fellow."

Curiously, Mrs. Granville didn't chastise Abby, when it seemed the perfectly natural thing for her to do, after being so vigilant about her other social "failings." Instead, I caught a sympathetic glance, followed by a crease of worry that didn't lift as she finished her portion. And after the custard had been served and eaten, she said, as if she'd been thinking of just how to phrase it, "I'm glad to see your spirits returning, Ruth. I'm sure your parents and grandparents will be happy to see your change, too, when you reunite, which Abby tells me might be more quickly than we'd anticipated since your deceased fiancé's sister is visiting your parents' ranch."

Not a whiff of her tone suggested I wasn't still a welcome guest. But she was clearly reminding me of my obligations to my parents. I remembered that Abby had said her mother struggled with how innocent Mr. Crane might be. It occurred to me that Mrs. Granville might worry what my family would think of her allowing me to become entangled in his case.

"You and Abigail are responsible for that change," I said. "You have been wonderful to me, and I'm enjoying learning about the city."

As we walked into the parlor to read and talk, Mrs. Granville looked at Abby. "You should show her your office, dear. Weren't you going to do that?"

Even Abby was surprised at her mother's mention of the newspaper. Prior to this, she'd been proud of Abby, yes, but had no inclination to lead another girl astray down the path of professional careers.

"Why, yes, of course," Abby stammered. "Tomorrow. I'll take you tomorrow, Ruth."

"That's a good idea," Mrs. Granville said.

"I'd hoped to check more churches, too," I said as we sat in the parlor. "For Ted's grandfather. Did you have any luck with that today, Abby?" I'd wanted to ask this at dinner, but her banter with her mother had made interruption difficult.

Abby shook her head. "Many weren't at home, and the few that were hadn't a thought who this mysterious preacher could be."

"I know so many in that community, it is more efficient if I handle it entirely," Mrs. Granville said. "I've already made inquiries and will continue doing so."

With that, the topic seemed to be closed, and we moved on to talking about music and books. But throughout the conversation, I was distracted, worried about Ted and also about my family's reaction to my involvement in his grandfather's case. Mrs. Granville's desire to have me accompany Abby instead of working with Ted churned up a muddy sea of doubt. By the time I went to bed, I found myself riven once more by conflicting emotions.

I started a new letter home but wasn't able to pen a word beyond "Dear Mother and Father..." My heart was overflowing with the story of the day, with Ted's struggle on behalf of his grandfather, of my own sympathy for his plight, of how heartbreaking it was to watch him go through this difficulty, and even of my own journey toward acceptance of Miguel's death and the need to move beyond it—words I knew my mother would be relieved to hear....

But not a syllable flowed from my pen. Mrs. Granville, with her very subtle questioning and nudging, had made me realize how much this relationship with Ted would hurt my family.

Maybe the best thing to do was to think of booking my train passage home. I could contact Sally Tucker in the morning to see if she wanted to accompany me, or I could just make the journey myself.

Oh, it wouldn't mean I was going to stay away from San Francisco forever. But it might be better to tell my parents about Ted's struggles in person, make them understand how the Billy Crane they knew was not the same one he was defending now. Assuming, of course, that he wasn't. Even Ted had had his doubts. I didn't know the man, so it was only natural for me to wonder, as well.

I stood looking out into the darkening twilight over the rooftops.

Yes, I could do all that in the morning. But I didn't want to. I wanted to stay here.

Chapter Ten

BY THE TIME ABBY and I met for breakfast in the dining room, Mrs. Granville had already departed. She'd left a note for her daughter, though, that, to me, communicated her mission:

> *I hope you girls have a wonderful day exploring your office, Abby, and showing Ruth more of the sights of San Francisco. Please use my tab at Delucca's for lunch, and this evening I've invited the rector of Church of the Trinity for dinner at seven. I might also suggest you go see Jane Stilwether, who is the niece of the minister who conducted the wedding of Ruth's grandparents. I know they'd be delighted to hear Ruth had met a member of the family present at her grandparents' marriage. I've sent a message that you might drop by. Here is the address...*

So, she'd pretty much scheduled us the full day, keeping the possibility of contacting Ted to a minimum. She was perfectly willing to help Ted, but she seemed to draw the line at encouraging a relationship between me and him.

If Abby understood that message, she didn't agree with it because she immediately began talking about how and when we would see Ted.

"No one will be in the office until late morning," she said, heaping her plate with eggs and sausage from the sideboard. "So I suggest we seek out Ted first thing. In fact…" She turned toward the kitchen and called for the housekeeper, who appeared in the door within moments.

"Stella, would you ask Jimmy to run a message to a Mr. Theodore Beaumont for me? He's at a boardinghouse. Here, I'll write it down." In an instant, she'd retrieved paper and pencil from a drawer and scribbled a quick note about plans to meet. Then she gave the folded missive to Stella with the boardinghouse address. Only then did she sit down to eat, untroubled by her now no-longer-warm breakfast.

"After we meet with Ted and find out what he's been up to, we'll do all the other things Mother has scheduled for us." She smiled. "I think Mother feels a bit negligent, leaving you to my devices alone. She must be feeling the need to demonstrate to your family she is taking good care of you."

I appreciated her frankness, but it made me crave more. "Do you think, Abby, that she is having misgivings about my…friendship…with Ted, given my family's history with his grandfather?"

Abby was neither hesitant nor offended. "I think it is entirely possible," she said between bites. "But I also think it doesn't matter. Ted should not be asked to carry the sins of his ancestors, even if he is defending one of them. He's well-intentioned, with a good heart, something I imagine good people would come to understand." She plowed back into eating with gusto, and her words made my appetite return, so I did the same.

We'd only been eating for a few minutes, though, when voices in the kitchen grabbed our attention.

"What—?" Abby said, standing. Before she'd had a chance to place her napkin on the table, though, the housekeeper opened the door to the dining room and announced:

"Mr. Beaumont is here."

Ted!

"Tell him to come in, come in," Abby said, gesturing. Then she looked at me and shrugged.

Ted stepped through the kitchen door to the dining room a second later, his hat in hand.

"I'm sorry to interrupt you," he said, looking from me to Abby.

"No interruption at all! We were going to come see you. Sit down and eat with us." Then, in a flurry, she went into the kitchen to tell Stella to tell Jimmy not to deliver our message, if he'd not already left.

"Good morning," Ted said shyly to me.

I returned the greeting, feeling oddly nervous, as if afraid he might find me…unattractive. How silly—I'd brushed and styled my hair that morning with care, and my outfit—the blue suit—was clean and neat. Unlike Abby's, I had to admit. Her brown jacket was missing a button, and the sleeve appeared worn at the elbows. Her cream-colored blouse was pretty but rumpled, as if she'd not seen to its being put away properly. And her hair—well, it was a wild storm, as usual. All these things made her all the more lovable to me now, however, and I didn't think to say a word about them to her.

When she returned to the room, she again insisted on Ted joining us for breakfast, and he agreed, placing his hat on a chair and sitting down himself while Stella fetched another plate.

"Why on earth did you come in the back way?" Abby asked, slathering jam on a piece of biscuit. "Is the road blocked out front?"

"No, no…I…well, truth be told, I came here to warn you—especially you, Ruth—and I didn't want anyone to follow."

My heart started racing, and Abby stopped eating mid-bite.

We all waited until Stella placed a plate and cutlery before him and left the room. Then he continued.

"Yesterday, when we were in the foothills, Ruth, I thought I saw something. I didn't want to alarm you, so I didn't say anything. And then, when we returned here, I had the curious sensation that someone was watching us. That was why I didn't want to linger. I also wanted to return to the hills, to see if, perhaps, my grandfather was right about hiding places…."

"Ted, how dangerous!" I'd suspected he might return, of course, but hearing him say he had was a giant step away from imagining same.

"It was risky, but I had a firearm and was confident I could overtake any scoundrel who tried to stop me."

"Oh, Ted, don't leave us in suspense. What did you find?" Abby asked.

He looked down. "Nothing. Nothing of…value," he said, glancing at me.

"But the scoundrel—did he follow you?" I asked, breathlessly. Despite my efforts to remain calm, I felt my pulse galloping.

"I led him on a course that eventually lost him," he said, smiling. "It was simple, really. I merely returned the horse to the stable, went to my boardinghouse, and left a few minutes later to resume my trek, being careful to look around me."

"Then why the secretiveness this morning?" Abby asked. "Did your follower reappear?" She stood, grabbed Ted's empty plate and began filling it with heaping helpings of everything available. Once done, she placed it in front of him with an expression that seemed to say, "I know you're hungry, so eat." He complied, talking between morsels.

"I wasn't sure—I didn't want to take a chance. I didn't think anyone was after me, but I certainly didn't want to lead them to this door if they were."

"If they saw you here yesterday," I offered, happy to see him eating so heartily, "they already know we are your accomplices."

Abby laughed. "Thank you, Ruth. I like the sound of that—accomplices." She grinned and looked at Ted. "Ruth is right—you needn't worry about us. But I'm glad you gave us a warning. I'll be watchful."

"I really don't think you'll be in any jeopardy, but I thought it safer not to be so blatant with my...friendship...with you, lest it put you at risk." He said this looking straight into my eyes, and I understood his meaning—that I was not to read indifference into his distance, should he not be coming around as frequently. My heart sank just a little. I was disappointed at this prospect.

"What do you think this all means?" I asked.

"I think—I hope—it means that I'm on the trail of the true culprits," he said with such a bright tone that it lifted my spirits. "My grandfather was clearly correct about the hideaways. So it's just a matter of finding the treasure from the robbery. And if my follower was involved, it's only a matter of time before he leads me to the stolen property."

"Ted! You mustn't do this on your own," I said, my fears for him rising. "It's too dangerous, whether you're armed or not. Besides, you'll need witnesses. You'll need someone from…from the law…to verify that you didn't plant the evidence and to help you find the true criminals."

"Ruth is right," Abby said with conviction. "You're no further ahead if you take the treasure into the police on your own. They'll assume your grandfather told you where to find it. You have to have a clear connection between it and the gang that did the heinous deed."

"Yes, I know," Ted said, eating heartily.

"We'll go with you—to the police chief. Or should it be a sheriff? Let's hope so. I have concerns about San Francisco's government and assume the police department is no more immune from corruption than city hall. Who is the lawman who would have control over this situation? I can find out. Someone at the paper would know. Good thing we're headed there first thing—"

Ted held up his hand, laughing. It was good to hear him laugh, a measure of how hopeful he felt now. "I'll take care of it. I promise you. I will not handle it on my own. But I will not allow either of you to be involved, either."

"We are involved!" Abby protested, rising to pour herself another cup of coffee and accidentally spilling some on the cuff of her blouse. She frowned for a moment, then ignored it and went on with her task. "And I'll not have you navigating the rocky shoals of our city's legal system without some help. If I am with you, I can say I'm with the newspaper. That will make sure whoever you deal with is inclined to do all that is honorable, lest their deeds be revealed to the world."

I concurred. "You helped me with my problem. Let us help you."

His eyes sparkled as he wiped his mouth with his napkin. As he set it by his now-empty plate, he appeared to be thinking over Abby's offer. But then he began to shake his head slowly. "I'm sorry, but I must decline...at least for the moment. I promise you I will take you up on your offer of help should I need it. But for now, I think it is in my interest and my grandfather's interest if I don't go in to the police with a threatening attitude, so to speak, which could make them less inclined—not more so, I'm afraid—to help me."

"Is that where you're headed this morning?" Abby asked.

"I'm going to file some legal papers, and I'm telegraphing the prison to ask about a doctor seeing my grandfather."

I suspected he wouldn't tell us if he were going to the police first, for fear Abby would insist we accompany him. But still, it bothered me that he wasn't immediately going to the authorities.

"What if the criminals suspect you're after them and move the treasure and run away? Wouldn't it be best to quickly take care of this aspect of the case?" I asked. In fact, why hadn't he gone last night or first thing this morning before coming to see us? Something didn't quite make sense.

His face reddened just a bit, and he didn't look at me before answering. "I have my reasons for doing it this way," he said softly. "But I assure you I'm handling it the best way possible, under the circumstances."

We finished our breakfast shortly, and, after some protests on Abby's part—that we accompany Ted or he go with us—we parted ways. Before heading out for his day's tasks, though, Ted managed to speak a few words to me alone while Abby went in search of a hat pin she couldn't find despite having used it just yesterday.

We stood in the parlor, and he surprised me by reaching for my hands.

"I would very much like, after this is all over, if you will consider letting me continue our friendship, Ruth," he said looking into my eyes. "I realize you are still recovering from a great sorrow, so your friendship is all I ask for at this time. And I also realize that your family might struggle to put behind them the bad memories of my grandfather's past behavior. I am patient, though, and I want you to know that I will wait for the moment that best suits your family and yourself. But, please, be patient with me, as well. I might not be able to see you often over the next few days, as I tend to what I hope are the finalities of this case."

His words knocked the wind right out of my chest. I didn't know what to say. I felt my face heat and my hands tremble under his strong grip. At last, just as Abby was whirling down the stairs, talking as she came, I whispered, "I would like very much to be your friend."

With a full heart, I left him, Abby and I striding toward downtown.

THE TRIP TO THE newspaper was so much more than I had imagined. I had expected it to be interesting, of course, but I ended it with a feeling of great admiration for Abigail and a new desire to learn more about this profession.

When we arrived at the tall building in the middle of town, I didn't know what I expected—maybe neat offices with clerks busily writing and machines clacking as pages were printed.

Instead, I found organized chaos, and with a smile, I realized this was Abby's world. No one here cared if she were disheveled. No one here cared if she wore yesterday's fashions that needed mending, or if her hair needed a good brushing and her face a splash of water to remove a smudge. Here, all they seemed to care about was her spirit and her mind. If anything, she was better groomed than a good portion of the employees I saw, scribbling away.

"'Morning, Miss Granville," a short, balding man in shirtsleeves said as we walked on to her floor. In his hand were sheets of paper and behind his ear was a pencil. "You should talk to Al. He has a job for you."

After making our introductions—this fellow was an editor of some kind, which surprised me when he wasn't more formally attired—Abby showed me where she worked, a desk as overflowing with papers as her head was with ideas. In the center was a big mechanical contraption—a typewriter. I'd never seen one and wanted her to show me how to use it, but she demurred.

"I type pretty quickly," she said under her breath, "while most of these fellows seem to take pride in not learning how to play these keys. If I'm not careful, they'll be handing me all their handwritten notes to type. I admit to some subterfuge—pretending to be as poor as they are on the typewriter. But I will happily show you how to use it when we have fewer people about to disturb us!"

Just as she finished her whispered conversation with me, a man approached who, like the editor we'd just met, did not stand on ceremony. His shirtsleeves were rolled up to his elbow, his collar undone, suspenders holding up trousers as rumpled as Abby's blouse. And in his hand was the stub of a cigar, barely lit. I guessed him to be around fifty. He had a full head of bushy hair the color of snow and a rugged face with dark eyebrows.

"Abby—get in my office. I've been waiting for you to show up!" No greeting for me, the idle stranger. I thought I should stay behind at Abby's desk, but she insisted I accompany her, telling me that "Al wouldn't mind or wouldn't notice," so I scurried past other untidy desks until we reached an office of sorts—an enclosure in the corner of this floor with windows of beveled glass looking out onto this news room.

Abby introduced us—Al was her section's editor—but the man just grunted and nodded while we sat down.

"This Italian songbird's in town or getting here soon—"

"Caruso," Abby helpfully supplied.

"Yeah, him. And I know the theater set is all agog over the whole visit by The Metropolitan Opera with Caruso being the icing on their cake." He spoke as fast and clipped as the taps of the typewriter, and at one point leaned back and put a shoe on the desk. I expected Abby to object, but she merely sat on the edge of her seat with a small notebook and pencil in her hand, ready to take notes.

"So we should be writing something about the parties they'll be throwing for this civilizing event," Al went on. "You know, the usual—who's hosting what, what Mrs. La-Di-Dah serves, what all the ladies are wearing."

"What about an interview with the tenor himself?"

"The what?"

"Enrico Caruso."

"Well, yeah, if you can get it. But I hear he's something of a lady's man, so I wouldn't be going alone.

Maybe Miss…Miss…" He pointed to me, but Abby refused to refresh his memory, and he eventually gave up trying to recall my name. "Maybe your friend here can go with you. Although it would be better to take a fellow with you. Got any fellows who could do that?" This last question was put forth in a rather snide tone, and if Abby wasn't offended, I certainly was. I had a mind to stand up and walk out of his office in a huff.

Abby, however, remained calm, although I could tell from her thinly pressed lips that she was not in a charitable mood toward her boss. She'd not written a single thing down and now merely placed the small notebook in a pocket, along with the pencil.

She stood, and I followed suit, but before leaving, she questioned her editor in a confident voice.

"You promised me that I could pursue the city hall corruption story, helping Peter with the job. Yet you've not given me one assignment," she said with a quiet strength. This was a different Abby from the cheerful one I was used to. She was resolute and serious. "I'll do my usual good work on this society story, Al, but it's not the best way to use a good writer, and you know I'm a good writer. I could find out things Peter can't. I have other sources. Someone will want the story, and I would hope it would be this paper." Not giving him a chance to reply, she turned and left.

I flushed with excitement and pride. I knew what her underlying message was. She'd threatened to uncover the story anyway and take it to a competitor if he wouldn't allow her to use her talents. I'd never seen such an exhibition. It made me…hungry…to be like her, to find something I truly wanted to accomplish and to go after it no matter what the opposition was.

When we got to her desk, she stopped and sat, urging me to do the same in the chair next to it.

"I'll be just a moment. I have to finish a piece I wrote the other day." With a quick glance around the room, she scrolled paper into her typewriter and began typing at a breakneck speed, her brow furrowed and her mouth downturned. Within a quarter hour, she was finished, and she called out for a "copy boy" to come pick up the piece before dusting her hands together, as if wiping dirt from them, and standing.

"Let's get going," she said, "before I can't control my temper any longer and do or say something I'll regret."

On the sidewalk a little while later, I asked her what the story was she'd just handed in, expecting to hear of some important piece of reportage that would set to rights a city ill or save an unjustly accused from prosecution.

"It was Mrs. Delilah Beewater's famous Lilac Time Lemon Coffee Cake recipe, which for decades she has refused to share, but due to my intrepid efforts as an investigative reportress of the first order, she divulged to yours truly. Now citizens of this fine town will not have to wait a single day longer to have this scoop delivered to their doorsteps, surely resulting in righteousness vanquishing evil and goodness triumphing over all." Her face reddened as she issued this sarcastic proclamation, and for the first time since being introduced to her, I understood the frustrations that a bright, clever girl like Abby faced as she tried to make her way in the world.

"I—I am sure it will be a fine piece," I said, not sure what else to offer.

At that, Abby laughed, her irritation melting in the spring sun. "I apologize. I shouldn't have drawn you into my own daily dramas. I enjoy them for the most part, and

I'm positive I will convince Al to give me more challenging work."

"I have no doubt you will!"

THE REST OF THE DAY was uneventful and fun. Lunch at Delucca's was a treat, and we did try to see the Mrs. Stilwether that Abby's mother urged us to visit, only to find she was not at home. We left a card saying we'd try again.

But throughout this breezy idyll of an afternoon, a voice kept whispering in my ear, disturbing my calm in a simmering way. All the voice said was: *Ted*. I kept hoping we'd run into him on our travels, a silly desire given how many people were in the city and how unlikely it would be for our paths to coincidentally pass.

He wanted to continue our "friendship," he'd said. It thrummed in my memory all day, now pushing aside my previous sadness, taking with it, too, the regrets and resentments I usually felt toward anyone who tried to rid me of my dour thoughts.

I was beginning to live again, fully live, stepping out of shadows into warm, embracing light.

Chapter Eleven

AT DINNER THAT NIGHT with the rector and his wife of Trinity Church, we learned that several itinerant preachers had been in the area recently, working mostly near the harbor. This news was delivered with a fair amount of scorn. It was clear to me that the pastor didn't think highly of such ministries and kept track of them when he could to discourage his flock from wandering to new leaders.

I must also admit to a general discomfort with this couple because of all the questions they asked about my background—about my father, that is, and "his kind." Even Mrs. Granville and Abby picked up on this thinly disguised condescension, either jumping in with glowing descriptions of my father's ranch—that they knew of only from my descriptions—or changing the subject.

After they'd left, a pale Mrs. Granville turned from the door and announced, "I sincerely apologize for my acquaintances' poor manners, Ruth. I shall think twice before inviting them again." The dear woman had been shaken by the incident, and I tried to set her mind at ease by being especially cheerful and grateful for her hospitality the next few days.

Ah, the next few days—a whirlwind of activity. With the information about the preachers, I was eager to investigate harbor environs, but Ted refused to let us do so. Those areas, he said, were too seedy for women, even accompanied by a strong man. He took it upon himself to look, unfortunately, finding nothing of value.

We had our hopes raised again, though, when we heard of a minister who was going to preach one morning at a nearby park. Mrs. Granville herself provided this tidbit, which she'd picked up on one of her pastorly visits.

Filled with excitement, Abby, Ted and I hurried to the park on a bright, cool morning, joining a small crowd, listening to a white-haired man talk of gloom and doom to come. "This city will fall," he shouted, clutching a Bible to his chest, "and all other cities of sin and waste!"

Abby clucked her tongue in approval of the denunciation of the city's corruption, although she was thinking of sins of greed, not of the flesh. Ted just grimaced and shook his head when it was clear this man didn't quite meet the description his grandfather had provided, and, besides, as Ted pointed out, his grandfather was unlikely to have been persuaded by a message so full of condemnation and so barren of grace.

As for me, well, I must admit to enjoying being in Ted's presence. He'd even dared to reach for my hand when we'd scurried to the park that morning, ostensibly to make sure I wouldn't fall as we rushed over uneven walks. But he'd kept holding it as we'd listened to the preacher storm and rage, and I felt warm with comfort and a new excitement at his touch. I was disappointed when he finally broke the connection at the end of the "performance" and announced he had some more leads to follow.

But after that morning, Abby and I had to hurry to meet Jane Stilwether, the niece of the minister who'd married my grandparents. She'd sent a note round suggesting this time, and we'd be rude to decline. Although the house wasn't far from us, I resented the time we'd have to spend there because I was eager to get back to helping Ted, even though I wasn't clear on how I could do that precisely, except to be in the same room with him discussing possibilities.

But it turned out that our meeting with Mrs. Stilwether was both heartwarming and fortuitous.

A short, compact woman of my parents' age, she welcomed Abby and me into a tasteful, small home on the outskirts of the Nob Hill neighborhoods. It sat on a steep hill that had left me breathless to climb, and seemed as narrow as it was tall. The front room boasted bright bay windows, though, from which one could see a glint of the harbor way in the distance.

A widow, Mrs. Stilwether lived quietly alone, venturing out for church functions and the occasional civic meeting, she told us. She was particularly interested in the city's history and was gathering materials for some articles on the days of the Gold Rush, when San Francisco began to teem with new emigres from elsewhere in the country.

While we sipped a fragrant tea in her parlor, she went into a back room and retrieved a box of mementoes, one of which was her aunt's journal.

"Knowing you were coming," she said to me as she opened the leather-bound book to a page marked with a pink ribbon, "I looked through this for something relevant." She handed me the precious book with its marked page.

And there I read of my grandparents' wedding in the parlor of her minister uncle's house so many years ago. After descriptions of the couple and those who stood up for them—including Abby's grandmother, Willa, and her grandfather, Josephus, she'd written:

> *Their loving spirits lifted my own. How could one not feel bathed in grace when in the presence of two who so clearly felt united in their souls? They'd been through great travails to reach this point, and I myself knew how that journey could deepen or corrupt affection. When Mr. Winchester looked at his young bride, it took my breath away, reminding me of my early wedded days when the excitement of new love provided the tiniest glimpse of the deep and serene joy that was yet to come....*

Tears filled my eyes, thinking of my grandparents so young and happy, a happiness almost stolen from them by the man I was trying to help Ted defend. I handed the book to Abby so she could read the description of Willa Barton, her grandmother: "tall and pretty in a sweet, simple way, a bit fragile from her recent birthing and the strains of the trip, but glowing with inner strength…" The birth had been Abby's uncle, now in Montana.

"Thank you," I murmured to Mrs. Stilwether. "My grandparents have told me their story, but this journal makes it come alive."

"My uncle ministered to the needy at the time, a vocation that I'm afraid became increasingly difficult as he grew older. He and my aunt ended up moving back East a few years after your grandparents came through. They were dedicated abolitionists, and he felt a calling to preach on it as the turmoil escalated," she said, referring to the War Between the States.

"What happened to them?" Abby said after clearing her throat. She, too, had obviously been moved by reading an account of her grandmother.

"Sadly, they were not long for this world after leaving California. They returned East by ship, first sailing to Panama, then taking the grueling overland journey to board a schooner up the coast. My aunt apparently became afflicted by malaria and died soon after they'd arrived in Maryland, where they'd determined to settle. After my uncle buried her, he himself lived but a year longer before dropping of a broken heart. But not before he'd preached up a storm, going from town to town on the Eastern Shore, to condemn slavery." She smiled. "From his letters to my parents—my father was his brother, you see—he had earned a reputation both good and bad, feared and welcomed."

Mrs. Stilwether's parents, it seemed, had come west right after the war, her father deciding that he could set up a mercantile in San Francisco to serve the growing population. He'd been right. His store had been prosperous, and he and her mother had lived comfortable lives until their passing about five years ago. She lived off the proceeds of the sale of the store, since her own husband had not been nearly as successful at his profession as a carpenter. "He built this home," she told us. "And it's built to last a lifetime. Too many people want something fast nowadays and not something sturdy."

Before we left, I couldn't resist asking her about the itinerant preacher, only divulging that he had helped an acquaintance on a matter of personal faith, and we'd like to find him.

To my shock, the woman nodded her head at the description.

"Yes, I think I have seen him. He was preaching near the wharf a week or so ago—I can't remember exactly. But it was a man of that description. A quite compelling speaker, too. I was there with a friend who had business with a shipper, and I had to wait a long time while she finished her task. He was a very persuasive and inspiring man, talking a great deal about forgiveness. Such a change from some of those men who talk nothing but fire and brimstone."

We questioned her more on his whereabouts but learned little else. Still, it was reassuring to hear at last that someone else had seen this mysterious preacher.

On the street outside, Abby squeezed my arm. "How resourceful you are, thinking to ask her about the preacher!" she exclaimed. "It hadn't occurred to me that she would know of him. She leads a rather restricted life here." She swept her arm around the quiet neighborhood. "We'll have to tell Ted. He'll be so pleased!"

AND TED *WAS* PLEASED…even though his elation was short-lived.

We saw him for dinner that evening—Abby insisted on inviting him, sending a message round to his boardinghouse. It took him awhile to get it, however, because it turned out he'd moved. When he shared this news with us, at first I thought it meant his circumstances had become more dire, but he informed us he'd been able to secure better quarters not so far from the Granvilles. I didn't know San Francisco well, but I knew it enough by now to realize this meant he was in a better neighborhood.

"Oh, that's wonderful," Abby said, wiping a splash of tea from her cuff as we ate dessert. "But it must cost a pretty penny. How much is the rent?"

"Abigail!" Mrs. Granville said before Ted could respond. "Personal questions such as that have no place in polite society."

"Mother, I was just trying to determine if Ted was getting a fair deal."

Ted laughed. "I assure you I am."

I smiled at him and noticed he was looking less…ragged. His shirt appeared to be new, and I'd observed him fingering what appeared to be a gleaming pocket watch, which had to have been a new purchase, as well. Curiosity tugged at me, but, as Mrs. Granville had said, personal questions, such as where he got the money for these things, were not polite. I might have been raised on a ranch, but my parents had instilled similar lessons in me and my brother.

"Have you been able to do any other legal work while you're here?" I asked instead.

"No, I'm afraid not. Although I have inquired at the offices of several attorneys, to see if they were looking for assistance of any kind."

"So you plan to stay on here, after your grandfather's case is settled?" Abby asked, then looked at her mother and said, "I don't think that's too personal a question, Mother. I think it demonstrates our interest in his well-being."

Mrs. Granville just frowned and sighed.

"It hadn't been part of my original plan, but lately, I have been thinking of staying here," Ted said, looking at me. "Perhaps even sending for my sister once I'm settled."

Blush warmed my cheeks.

"And with this new information from Mrs. Stilwether, I am much more hopeful that we'll find my grandfather's alibi witness. At the very least, a sworn affidavit from her might get me another extension in order to resume searching for the preacher," he added.

Mrs. Granville grimaced and shook her head a little. "I don't want to dash those hopes—I hesitated to say this when the girls first told me the story—but Jane Stilwether has had a reputation of late, as she gets older that is, to embellish stories."

"Mother! Who is the one making personal comments now?" Abby chided.

"As I said, Abigail, I hesitated before mentioning this. But if Theodore intends to get a sworn statement from Jane, he should know of the perils of that strategy."

My heart sank for Ted. "What precisely do you mean by her tendency to 'embellish' stories, Mrs. Granville?" I inquired.

"Jane is a dear woman who does much good," Mrs. Granville said. "But after her husband passed, her loneliness has led to a vivid imagination. When she hears someone talking about a gathering or a place or an event, she will often speak as if she had personal knowledge of such things. I believe she likes to imagine she was there—she and her husband used to socialize quite a bit—and truly thinks her fantasies are reality. Those who have affection for her, as I do, happily tolerate this…shortcoming."

So Mrs. Stilwether might not have seen the preacher, after all, but might, instead have just been caught up in our story, wanting to be a part of it. I looked at Ted. His face registered what I, too, felt—terrible disappointment.

"Oh, dear," was all Abby, usually effusive, could offer. Then, after an awkward silence, "Don't worry, Ted. We'll keep looking."

Mrs. Granville's news put a damper on the end of our meal, and we all were quiet and even a bit glum when we retired to the parlor where Mrs. Granville again prevailed upon Abby to play the piano for us. There was less argument this time but still enough to give me some time to talk with Ted alone, and my curiosity had to be sated.

"You seem to be doing well," I said. "I'm glad you are enjoying better circumstances."

He nodded but looked down, as if embarrassed. "Thank you. I—"

"Oh, Ted, you don't want to hear Beethoven again, do you?" Abby interrupted.

"Whatever you want to play will be delightful," he responded.

"What did the police say when you talked to them about the hiding place?" I pressed.

He reddened, again uncomfortable. "I didn't go to them. I—I took Abby's words to heart. I don't want to end up making more trouble for my grandfather than he's already in by happening upon a policeman who is less than honest."

We didn't talk after that as Abby had started playing, but as I listened to her beautiful—if dramatic—rendering of Schubert pieces, I was troubled. Ted had shown up at Abby's house visibly better off—a new shirt, a new watch—and had admitted to finding more expensive living quarters. He'd come into some money.

And it was shortly after he'd thought he might have come upon a thieves' hideaway. With a start, I remembered that he'd told me a gold watch had been among the items stolen. Disappointment and suspicion clouded my mood, darkening the rest of the evening for me. By the time I went to bed, I felt lower than I had before being lifted out of my sadness over Miguel. I'd possibly betrayed his memory with someone not worthy of my affection.

Chapter Twelve

MY HEART STILL troubled, I accompanied the Granvilles to church on Sunday.

To my surprise, when we entered the bright, airy church, Ted was already there, sitting in a pew near the front. Abby hastened to sit next to him, and he stood and smiled warmly at me when we approached.

It was just as well we couldn't exchange any words, however, because I had been unable to get off my mind the suspicions that had begun to grow there. Was it possible that Ted had found the loot from the robbery and taken it himself to better his circumstances?

It horrified me to think this. First, I'd grown fond of Ted. I'd even begun to hope that our friendship might deepen. Here was a man who was strong and smart, who seemed to love life and his own small family, whose bright mind moved as swiftly and surely as Miguel had moved on a horse—why, Ted had made me leave some of my sorrow over Miguel behind! I'd not thought that at all possible.

But secondly, I was troubled by the fact that I might have so misjudged his character—if he were guilty of the sins I was imagining. Was I so protected and naïve that I would not recognize a swindler? Ted, after all, came from a family with a notorious criminal at the head. Perhaps Ted had inherited some of those same evil proclivities?

These thoughts darkened my heart as the hymns began and the prayers followed. And then the preacher, a tall man in his early forties, rose. His words seemed aimed at my heart.

He had chosen a deep subject—original sin, the fall from the garden—and he talked of Eve's role in tempting Adam, but not in a way that stirred my blood against him. It seemed to me that far too many men were eager to blame women for their downfall. But this minister took a different tack, making it clear as day that Adam had been the "architect of his own fate, with his own free choices. And that is God's gift to us—the free will that allows us to steer our course in life. It's a gift fraught with peril, with responsibility and even with temptation. But ultimately, it is our life, our actions, that we will be judged by, not to whom we were born or with whom we associate...."

He went on to preach about how easy it was to make broad assumptions about groups of people, and here I nodded my head mentally as I thought of the railroad agents and the minister and his wife who'd seen me as a member of a "tribe," more than as an individual.

But I also reflected on how easy it was to fall into this thinking in other ways, how I was now beginning to do the same thing with Ted—seeing him as an extension of his grandfather, who had been a villain at one point in his life. Whether he still was one was immaterial. I could not judge Ted by his grandfather's sins.

I glanced at Ted. Today he wore one of his older shirts, neatly pressed but frayed at the cuffs. I glimpsed the pocket watch chain. There had to be an explanation for his newfound money. I merely had to ask...regardless whether the question was "personal."

And ask I did, as we sipped lemonade in the church yard after the service.

"I was admiring your watch the other day," I said. "It reminds me of one my grandfather has." This was truth—Grandfather Daniel did have a lovely piece, engraved and polished, a present from Grandmother one year.

He looked down, a pale blush covering his face. "Thank you. It was an unexpected gift...from a distant relative."

This was hardly a comprehensive answer, but I sensed he was uncomfortable talking about it, which made me afraid to press the issue. So I moved on to praising the preacher's sermon.

Although Ted nodded his head, he disagreed with the full lesson. "Sometimes I think it's nearly impossible to outrun one's legacy, though. It seems to nip at one's heels when least expected."

"Ted, you can't believe that we're to be judged by what our ancestors have done."

"Perhaps not judged as guilty but, rather, lacking in some way." He looked into my eyes, and I saw pain in his. What was he trying to say, that he'd found weakness in himself and been unable to avoid temptation?

"We're all lacking, to one degree or another," I continued, hoping he would divulge the source of his troubled mind.

This, at least, brought an ironic smile to his mouth. "Comforting thought, Ruth. That we are all lacking."

I laughed. "I didn't mean to offend...."

"No offense taken. It's good to remember that perfection is only possible in the next life."

Abby and Mrs. Granville joined us, introducing us to more of their friends, and then we left Ted and the church for a delightful midday meal and quiet afternoon, during which I wrote Mother and Father again—I was communicating more with them here than I did on the ranch. I resolved to be a better daughter when I returned home.

Writing to them reminded me of Anita's visit, and I realized I'd not thought about that since first hearing the news of her arrival.

THE NEXT WEEK I saw Ted only twice. He had a hearing on his grandfather's case and had to prepare, he told us, and he was pursuing the leads on the preacher, even if Jane Stilwether's word was unreliable.

I found myself missing him but also wondering if he was avoiding me. Had I touched on a sore subject when asking about the source of his newfound wealth?

I confided my misgivings to Abby on an excursion into town one day to pursue the Caruso social story. We were visiting a scion of San Francisco society, and Abby was all too happy to have me in tow—"at least one of us will look respectable," she'd said while trying to pat her unruly hair into place. I wasn't so sure. She might look past my darker skin and hair, but higher society types might not.

As we took a carriage to the house in question, I mentioned Ted's new circumstances and how he'd only mentioned he'd received some gifts from a distant relative.

"It seems to make him uncomfortable," I said.

"Yes, it does," Abby responded. "I think Ted feels very bad about the harm his...family...has done. He mentioned to me on Sunday that his grandfather is, in fact, penning a note of apology to your family and to my mother. Did he tell you that?"

"No," I said. "I didn't know."

"He might not have wanted to get your hopes up, but I think Ted is pretty confident his grandfather will provide one. I'm hoping that makes Ted feel a bit better about himself, actually."

"Why should Ted feel bad when his grandfather was the criminal?" I thought of the minister's sermon on Sunday.

Abby twisted her mouth to one side, then spoke. "I don't think he feels guilty so much as he worries that others might think poorly of him. It's …well, I'm taking a liberty here…you might sometimes feel the same way for different reasons. You have seen how some people are really base about your ancestry, and it probably sets you on edge at times."

Such as now, I thought ruefully as we pulled up in front of a rococo mansion. Would its owner assume I was Abby's maidservant? Did Ted feel that way—that those he met who knew of his grandfather's history would wonder if he was up to a task or about to take advantage of them?

With shame, I realized I had wondered that very thing— if he had followed his grandfather's path by finding and keeping the treasure from the robbery himself.

How hard it was to let go of such notions!

I put that aside, however, as we approached Abby's task at hand—learning just who was inviting the famous Italian tenor to soirees during his appearance in town.

BY THE END OF the day, I was thoroughly schooled in what it took to be a reportress. Abby might have chafed at her assignment—and it did seem very superficial to me, as well—but she pursued it with a dogged determination, as if it were a story critical to the lifeblood of the city. She interviewed society matrons right and left, never shirking from arriving on their doorsteps unannounced and asking them the blunt questions she needed in order to seek out who was providing what entertainment for Caruso and who was just hoping to catch his attention.

By the time we were done, I was fatigued in ways I'd never experienced on the ranch, even after a hard day of labor with my father and Joe. I was also filled with admiration for Abby and told her so when we reentered the Granville house late that afternoon.

"I know it's a trivial story," Abby said, unpinning her hat in the foyer. "But Al has to learn that I do a good job, regardless what the job is. I still intend to pursue the corruption tale, whether he wants me to or not."

We parted ways to rest and freshen up, I with a tentative hope in my heart that Ted would be joining us. If I saw him, perhaps I'd be able to put misgivings aside.

I was disappointed on that score, though, as I learned when the housekeeper handed me several letters after I roused from a brief nap.

Sitting in the parlor, I read the one from Ted first.

Dear Ruth, I'm sorry I won't be seeing you a great deal this week as I tend to my grandfather's business. I would like to ask you to dine with me one evening, if it is not too much of an imposition. Abigail could join us, as a chaperone, if you like. I leave that arrangement up to you.

I include with this note a letter my grandfather has written. I know you will decide what is best to do with it, but I hope it brings some peace to you and your family...

With trembling fingers, I opened the folded paper Ted had enclosed with his own note. Written in pencil on smudged paper in a quavering script, it was brief.

Dear Winchester Family,
I'm heartily sorry for the pain I caused you over the years. I hope that my past bad deeds haven't lingered long in memory, but that don't make them any less wicked. I should have apologized a long time ago, but I am not so ill mannered that I wouldn't know the feelings that a letter from the likes of me might stir up. You have had your own lives to lead, and I am not welcome in them. I know that. I'm not asking for your forgiveness because it seems to me that's an awful big request after what I'd done years ago. I beg the Almighty for His absolution, but I understand if you can't find it in your hearts to offer yours. It's nothing against you. If I could live my life over again, I'd have done a thousand things different, including how I treated you good people. It pains me that I didn't get to know you as the good people you are, and I carry that burden, among many, as punishment for my many sins. I sincerely hope you have lived lives of great happiness, undimmed by memories of my terrible acts. Again, I am deeply sorry for the pain I must have caused you by my reckless use of the gift of life God had given me. Sincerely, William T. Crane."

What a letter—I didn't know what to do with it. He was correct, of course—what right did he have to ask for forgiveness from my grandparents, if what I'd been told about him was true? He'd tried to injure them grievously, even unto death. But the fact that he recognized that, that he could understand how asking for their forgiveness was too much to ask of anyone, given the circumstances…it bespoke a humbled man, someone aware at last of his place in the world.

But how would my family react to receiving such a note? For that, I opened the next letter, which was from my mother. I almost immediately had my answer.

Dear Ruth, I cannot tell you the upset it has caused to hear you have been in contact, if only in a second-hand way, with Mr. William Crane. When I mentioned this to your grandparents, they were both disturbed and fearful for your safety. While we cannot judge his grandson from so far away, nor is it right to cast aspersions on the kin of a criminal, we think it would be best if you could come home as soon as possible, staying away from this situation altogether. We trust the Almighty will help confer justice on Mr. Crane, whether it is in the form of acquittal or, sad to contemplate, execution. We cannot be a part of these matters. When you come home, I will share with you the horrible stories— almost too awful to contemplate—that your grandmother told me about this man. If you knew them, you would not have been so quick to form a friendship with his grandson or aid in his work to clear his grandfather. It has clearly disturbed your grandmother, and this, in turn, upsets me. …

The letter went on for quite some time like that. And by its end, it was stained with my tears. How selfish I felt! And what a web of conflict I was now caught in! I stood and went to the front window, peering out at a quiet street scene. Few people were about. But the city, with all its wonderful and fearful possibilities, hummed just beyond this serene neighborhood. My excursion today had whetted my appetite for learning to make my own way in the world, like Abigail. How curious it was to think of the life I'd planned for myself with Miguel—it would have been the very domestic one my mother led, which I, to my shame, had often scorned. I'd wanted to be a full partner with Miguel on our ranch one day— helping him as I'd helped father and Joe. And yet, my life probably would have become increasingly restricted by the duties of motherhood and housekeeping.

Abigail, however, didn't notice housekeeping—even, I smiled at the thought, personal "housekeeping" of one's clothes and appearance. But I also suspected she'd be happily married to the right man, a man who respected her in the full—her mind and spirit.

As I pondered these things, she appeared in the doorway.

"Oh, dear. You look upset. Did you get a letter, too?" In her hand was a folded note similar in paper to the one I'd received from Billy Crane.

"Yes," I said, brushing away stray tears and turning back into the room, where we both sat on opposite divans.

"Mother's not in yet—that's how I ended up reading ours first."

"What are you going to do with it?" I asked.

"Why, give it to her, of course." She peered at me. "You don't think we have any choice, do you?"

"It…it occurred to me that these letters, as heartfelt as they are, will probably open old wounds," I said softly.

"Oh, I agree on that completely. But I think hiding them would be a grave disservice to both Mr. Crane and our families."

"How so?"

"If he's sincere—and I do believe he is—who are we to judge whether our families should see them? I mean, Ruth, that we really have no right to deny our families making the same judgments—for good or ill."

I sighed and nodded. I feared my family's reaction would be "ill." I had a hard time, after reading Mother's note, imagining she'd welcome Mr. Crane's letter or be willing to believe its sincerity.

"You're right," I said. "I should go write my parents immediately and enclose Mr. Crane's letter." As I turned to head back to my room, the front door opened and Mrs. Granville returned. Seeing us in the parlor, she offered a cheery greeting while removing her gloves.

"I hope you two had a lovely day," she said, smiling.

"Thank you. I enjoyed it a great deal," I said. "Abigail is a very skillful reportress. I learned a tremendous amount from her today." And then I excused myself, to tend to my letter, leaving Abigail alone with her mother. As I walked up the stairs, I heard Abby say, "Mother, I have something you should read."

I DON'T KNOW WHAT Abby said to her mother about Mr. Crane's note, but I wrestled with how to find the right words to use with mine. I toyed with the notion of simply penning a few lines, telling her what the note was, and leaving it at that.

But her own letter to me weighed heavily on my mind. She'd be expecting to hear my plans. Specifically, when I'd be returning home.

And this was when I decided on my path. I wouldn't send Mr. Crane's letter to her. I would deliver it in person when I returned home. There was no need to add to her worries.

And worry she would when she received my letter, because I filled it with the frankness Abby and her mother had demonstrated to me over these past few days. I told her that, although the business with the railroad agent had been successfully conducted, I felt I couldn't leave quite yet until I'd satisfactorily repaid young Mr. Beaumont for his aid. This might include, I told her, trying to help him find the preacher who'd provide the alibi for his grandfather.

"I know this will pain you, Mother, but I also know that you would want me to do what is right. And helping Mr. Beaumont in this very small way is the right thing to do after he helped me so kindly and so expertly. I realize his grandfather did great harm to our family many years ago. But Mr. Beaumont himself is above reproach, a courteous and intelligent gentleman. I…"

Here I paused, my hand hovering over the page before I continued.

"…I like him a great deal and think you would, too. But please do not concern yourself too much on my behalf. I hope to satisfy my sense of obligation soon and be home before Anita and her family depart."

Whether I liked it or not, I had to make preparations to leave soon. I needed to face the truth in my own situation. I was lingering because I liked it here. I enjoyed Abby and was learning from her a different approach to life, a cheerful honesty, a forthrightness, and a different path for a woman.

And I also liked Ted. A great deal, I realized. I'd miss him terribly if I left.

That affection, however, was tinged with doubt, about his new financial circumstances, about his grandfather. If I were to pursue a …friendship…with Ted, I had to first put those doubts to rest. And, resolving his grandfather's case would also bring peace to my family in some small way. Oh, it wouldn't atone for what he'd done to them years ago. But it would, I hoped, help them realize he had changed, and his grandson had not been cut from the same twisted cloth.

What a muddle my thoughts were as I tried to uncover this new "honesty" with myself! I hoped I was doing the right thing. I hoped I wasn't falling back into selfish ways, finding rationalizations for what I wanted to do anyway.

No, no, my obligation was to my family first, and I *would* fulfill it. I'd return home very soon, before Anita and her husband left. And I'd resolve my doubts about Ted and his grandfather in some way before that. I had to.

I would accept Ted's invitation to dine this week at which I'd tell him my intention to return home sooner rather than later.

I would enjoy seeing Anita. At least that buoyed my spirits.

MY WORRIES ABOUT my family's reaction to Billy Crane's letter were affirmed for me at the dinner table that evening. There was the usual sparring session between mother and daughter, but this time it was a more serious discussion, with none of the gratuitous, if fun, pokes at each other. Instead, we all debated the sincerity of Mr. Crane's apology.

"I have to admit that I'm glad my mother wasn't here to read it," Mrs. Granville said after a round of talk. She served herself some fruit and sipped at her tea after dinner. "I think it would have dug up a great deal of hurt she'd put behind—the memories of fearing Mr. Crane on the trail. She told me the stories when I was older even though I had been there, of course, as a young girl. I wanted to know, as I grew up, what had happened. It was as if I were putting pieces of a puzzle together."

"But Grandmama Willa wasn't the victim of Mr. Crane's misdeeds, was she?" Abigail asked gently.

"No, but she—and I—witnessed them. When your grandfather was shot by Mr. Crane, Ruth—oh, my, but I prayed as I'd never done before. He'd been such a sure, gentle leader to us all on that trek. And even though it felt more adventure than dangerous journey to me, deep inside I knew that without our wise guide, we would have found the trail difficult. Suddenly, it was unclear to me at that moment, the last weeks on the trail, if we would make it, after all. I think that incident made me grow up in some ways, see the world more clearly, see that there were dangerous people in it." She sipped more of her tea, lost in reflection. "Later, I learned of the other things he'd tried to do—helping to set up a kidnapping of your grandmother, luring your grandfather into a trap. Sadly, it didn't shock me by that point. I'd begun to see him as a personification of evil."

"No one is that, Mother. We're all capable of redemption," Abigail protested.

"That's true, dear. And I believe it with all my heart. But what his letter does…it's as if he's asking me to bestow that redemption on him. It's not mine to give."

"I'm afraid this is my fault," I rushed to say. Throughout their talk, I'd been feeling increasingly guilty. "I   thought that a letter of apology might be…helpful. I didn't realize, until I saw it, the kind of pain it would cause."

"Ruth," Abby said quickly, "don't for one moment think this is your fault. You are not responsible for the hurt he caused years ago, and I myself wouldn't have realized that a letter of apology can stir up as much pain as peace. I, too, thought it was a good idea."

"I must admit," I said, "I've now doubted whether to send it to my parents at all. I've seen the pain it's caused you. I don't want to inflict that on them. And I'll be returning home soon, putting their minds at ease."

While Mrs. Granville remained silent at this news, Abby immediately protested. "Returning home soon? Oh, no, Ruth! I'd hoped you'd stay longer. We have the opera to go to—Mother secured tickets—and you'd seemed interested in the reporting work. There's more to show you…."

"Abigail, Ruth has family obligations to consider. I'm sure her parents are eager to see her. It's the first time she's been away for so long." She quickly glanced at me. "That's not to say you are not welcome, Ruth. But I want you to be comfortable here, not worrying about your parents."

And not worrying my parents about my involvement with the grandson of an unsavory man. I sighed heavily.

"Mr. Crane doesn't ask anything of our families in his letter," I timidly offered, knowing her concern. "He doesn't even ask forgiveness, probably knowing it was not his to ask for."

"Or because he's too arrogant still to know he should ask for it," Mrs. Granville said.

"Mother!"

"Well, that's the problem, isn't it? We can't know what is in his heart at all. Only God knows that, and only God can judge him."

"I wish…" I began, hesitating to suggest such an idea. "I wish one could stare into his eyes and try to judge his sincerity."

"Men can lie as easily to your face as in writing," Mrs. Granville said.

"Oh, Mother, Ruth has a point. If the man is contrite, sincerely contrite, it would be easier to tell if you could see him face-to-face."

"I shudder at that thought!" Mrs. Granville said, pushing her dessert plate away. "It's bad enough he's reentered our lives through—"

"Through Ted," Abby finished for her. "Oh, please, don't tell me you are passing the sins of the grandfather onto the grandson. We all know better than that"

Mrs. Granville rose, her voice shaky as she spoke. "You're right, Abigail. I shouldn't do that. I must admit, however, that it's been a struggle not to pass that judgment since Ted has come here and I've had time to…think about things, to remember. It was so easy to open our doors to him at first, but then as time went on and memories returned…. Well, I pray about it daily. I don't wish Ted ill in any way. If his grandfather is innocent, I hope he is able to prove it before it's too late. But I have come to wish I didn't have to know of his predicament. Please excuse me, now. I have a fearful headache."

Abby rushed to ask her mother if she needed anything but returned to the dining room when her mother assured her she'd be fine.

"Oh, Abby, we've been selfish, indulging in this business with Ted."

"Nonsense, Ruth. It's not selfish to try and help another soul. Even Mother knew that—that's why she so quickly acted hospitable toward Ted." She grew thoughtful. "I can understand how Mother feels now, however, and I am sorry to have introduced this pain into her life." She smiled. "It's easy to have a burst of charitable feeling, isn't it? The hard part is sustaining it. Mother and I both struggle with this."

"One way or another, it will be over soon," I said.

"I'm afraid so."

With that, she moved on to another topic—my departure. She convinced me to stay until at least Caruso's performance, and I promised her I would.

Exhausted after the afternoon's emotional turmoil, I went to my room where I again rewrote my letter to my parents, telling them of my travel plans, how I'd try to determine if Sally could travel with me, and saying not a word more about Ted or his grandfather. I placed the letter of apology in with my personal things. It was something I decided I needed to hand them in person.

In person. After I saw someone else in person, so I could look him in the eye and try, for my family's sake, to gauge his sincerity.

I would talk to Ted about taking me to San Quentin to visit his grandfather.

Chapter Thirteen

As I SUSPECTED, going to see Mr. Crane at San Quentin proved a daunting task. First, I had to convince Ted, which was no easy matter. I decided to do so at our dinner together, several nights later. Abigail accompanied me to the restaurant, promising her mother she'd look after me, but then discreetly leaving me at the door to "finish some work at the newspaper office." I knew it was a ruse to allow Ted and me time alone together, and I was appreciative.

I'd fussed about my appearance before arriving at the small, but elegant hotel restaurant near the center of town. I chose my green velveteen suit and decided to forgo a hat, instead twisting my long plait into a bun, intertwined with a seed pearl strand from my mother. I'd patted lavender perfume behind my ears and fretted over whether my gloves weren't clean enough. I was as nervous as a new kitten away from the litter.

My heart palpitating wildly, I scanned the dining room from the lobby. Just as a maître d' headed my way to ask me if I'd like a table, Ted appeared, striding toward me from a seat in the far corner of the lobby.

"Ruth, thank you so much for meeting me. I wish you would have let me come round to pick you up. It would have been no trouble. You came alone?" He looked around.

"Yes. Abigail…had to write something…at her office…she'll meet me later," I said, stammering. I suddenly felt like a very young girl, unable to find words. When he touched my arm to lead me to a table following the maître d', I blushed and was embarrassed by the warmth surely coloring my neck and cheeks.

"You look beautiful tonight," he said in a hushed tone as he held my chair for me.

"Thank you. You look very dashing, too." And he did. He had on a new suit—another indication of better circumstances. A frown creased my brow, piercing my expectant mood. I so hoped his new money wasn't the result of something…unseemly.

"I'm happy you asked me to this dinner," I said after we'd looked over the menus and ordered. "I have two pieces of news that I need to share. I am booking my train trip home…very soon." I couldn't bring myself to tell him I was thinking of leaving the day after the Caruso program. It hurt me as much as it seemed to trouble him.

His face froze and an injured look darkened his eyes. After swallowing, he reached out impulsively and touched my hand on the table.

"Oh, Ruth, how that saddens me. I'd hoped…." He looked down nervously.

My heart quickened. Yes, it saddened me, too. I didn't really want to go, not in my heart of hearts. But I couldn't stay here indefinitely, and I couldn't disregard my mother's request for my return.

He looked up, keeping his hand on mine. "I actually asked you here tonight to plead my case." He smiled. "We've only known each other a short time, but you are a sweet and courageous woman I'd like to know more. With your permission, I'd like to write to your parents to ask if I might pursue a deeper…friendship…with you."

Now I smiled in return, happiness flooding me. He'd already mentioned his desire to be friends with me, but asking permission from my parents meant that he desired to become even more than friends. It showed he was a gentleman. "Oh, Ted, I'd like that very much. You should know that I will miss you terribly when I leave. I've not met anyone like you, not since..." I stopped myself. I had been about to say, "Miguel."

Ted understood and beamed. "I'm so flattered you think of me in that way, Ruth. You should know the sentiment is returned a hundredfold. I would very much like my sister to meet you."

Our dinners arrived shortly after this, creating an interlude of eating and chatting, a blissful half hour of comfortable peace, both of us secure in our mutual affection. Ted was asking to "court" me, and I knew where such courtships usually ended, at the altar. The thought lifted me up enough to push worries about my family's reaction aside. It's thrilling for any young woman to know that a man is enamored with her. But in my case, the feeling was returned, making it all the more wonderful, and it was a feeling I'd not expected to encounter again after Miguel. Ted had opened my eyes to the future. I felt fresh and new, as if life were starting over. In that glow of acceptance, it was hard for doubts to cast shadows.

"After my grandfather's case is over, I was wondering if I might arrange a visit to your ranch," Ted said as we started our desserts.

"I'd like that very much," I answered. "There's so much to show you, and, of course, you'd get to meet my parents and grandparents."

With the uttering of those words, reality finally dampened my exuberance. My grandparents. How would they feel meeting Ted? As my conversation with the Granvilles the other evening illustrated, the memory of what his grandfather had done could spring to life in hurtful ways. His very presence might prove wounding, especially if he looked like his grandfather.

"I want to meet your grandfather, too," I said simply.

"What?" His eyes widened. He looked confused.

"I want you to take me to San Quentin to meet him," I said.

"Ruth, no. It's no place for a woman. I can't allow that…."

"I have to see him, Ted. I have to look into his eyes. I have to see for myself if…"

He sighed, placed his napkin on the table. "You want to see if he's truly sorry for what he did."

"I have to. I have to be able to tell my parents and my grandparents that I saw with my own eyes, that I judged him myself."

He studied me for a long few minutes, worry shining in his eyes. "You don't believe his letter of apology."

"Yes, I do." I paused. "I think I do. Even you admitted to moments of doubt, Ted. I know my family will feel the same, the effect magnified. If I can tell them that I saw the man, that I looked into his eyes and judged, what I could, from such an encounter, they'd—"

"Be more accepting of me?" he interrupted. "I'm sorry, Ruth, but I think the last thing your family would want would be me introducing you to the man who caused them so much grief so long ago." He smiled sadly for a moment. "And I do not want to get off on the wrong foot with them. I appreciate your wish to see him for yourself, but a prison? What would they think of me if I endorsed that?"

I leaned into the table. "Oh, Ted, I have to. I plan on giving them the letter in person—not mailing it—and I want to be able to answer their questions about it all. And I want them to think kindly of you, too! I will make it clear this visit is my idea and you protested. But..."

"No 'buts,' Ruth. I can't allow it."

"You can't allow it?" Those words ignited a flame. "But you don't control me." Not even Miguel had controlled me.

"It's at least a day's journey! One of the reasons you've not seen me much this week is because I've had to make that journey twice. You can't do so without a chaperone. Who would you go with?" At the look in my eye, he groaned slightly. "No, not Abby. Her mother would be infuriated, too, and rightly so, that I'd allowed the both of you to go there."

"I traveled a farther distance to get here from Carmel Valley," I said, "with a woman I hardly knew. Abby and I could make the journey, stay at a respectable inn, and return the next day. We could accompany you on your next visit."

"How on earth would you convince Abigail's mother to endorse this journey?" he said, astonishment in his voice. At least he'd moved away from outright opposition, I thought with a small sense of triumph.

"I'm not sure, but if anyone can, it's Abby." Of course, I'd first have to convince Abby of the rightness of this mission.

Ted just shook his head. "I'm going to see him next Tuesday. I was going to tell Mrs. Granville and you and Abby that I can't attend the opera after all because of it. I have a visit with the warden scheduled to go over medical treatment for my grandfather."

"Then, that's when we'll go with you!" I leaned into the table. "Ted, you can't stop us. We're not asking your permission, just informing you of our intent." How easily I included Abby in this plan without even consulting her—who was the controlling one now?

He sighed, shook his head, looked down and away. Finally, after a long pause, he stared into my eyes, worry narrowing his own. "I can't forbid you to accompany me—that's true. But I'll do everything in my power to stop you should Abby not be available to come with you or should Mrs. Granville object. I'll give you a note to give to her tonight, informing her of my objections," he said.

And he wrote the note right there, pulling out a small leather-bound booklet, again something new and expensive-looking, and quickly writing the letter. After folding it, he handed it to me.

"The only reason I won't confront her myself is because I don't want to disturb her too late in the evening," he said. "And she might want to take in this news without me hovering nearby."

As he finished his missive, Abby herself strode into the lobby.

"I see I timed my work just right," she said, smiling as she approached us. "The citizens of San Francisco will be able to read in the morning of all the wonderful soirees our 'backward' town has planned for the great Caruso." She looked at me. "I hope you had a good evening, but it's probably time to chaperone you home, Ruth."

Ah, yes, the chaperone. I stood, as did Ted.

"I'll accompany you, as well," he said. "It should be a pleasant evening."

And it was. We strolled most of the way, after using a cable car for part of the trip. This time, I wasn't afraid but invigorated, breathing in the cool evening air, Ted's presence warming me. He surreptitiously reached for my hand and held it. I didn't want the ride to end.

But when it did, he still managed to find my hand as we walked toward the Granville home, Ted using the time to explain to Abby how I wanted to go to San Quentin to see his grandfather and how he opposed the trip and wouldn't allow it unless someone accompanied me—other than him, of course—and that if that person were to be Abigail, he couldn't possibly endorse the plan without her mother's agreement.

Abby enthusiastically nodded her head to everything except this last bit. She completely understood my desire to see Mr. Crane and didn't pause a second when this hitherto unrevealed scheme of mine was brought up. But at her mother's "permission," she objected.

"It's very polite of you to inform my mother, but I could do it on my own. She doesn't control my comings and goings, and I've wanted to view the big prison at some point, for my reporting career. I've heard rumors about its management that make one wonder…. As to the opera—I'm sure she can find some worthy members of her church to share the tickets with, and I'll reimburse her for her generosity."

I smiled. Abby was a ball of positive energy, ready to use anything to try to do good.

"I wouldn't want your mother to think I suggested this trip in any way," Ted said. "Or that I even think it's a good idea. I put that in my note. As for the tickets—I can't allow you to reimburse your mother. It's my fault if you don't go. I'll pay for them."

I nearly gasped—how expensive that would be!

"But you know we'd go to San Quentin anyway, right? With or without your permission." Abby asked.

"I put that in the note, too," Ted countered.

Chapter Fourteen

WHATEVER TED HAD put in his note, it wasn't enough to soothe Mrs. Granville's worries. But at least he seemed to have avoided her blame—she focused all her ire on Abby.

Before even finishing her coffee the next morning, she looked up at her daughter and exclaimed, "You cannot do this to me."

"Mother, who is doing what to you?"

"You know how much I will worry about you both on such a journey. And Ruth—I answer to her family for her safety and well-being. You can't ask me to give my blessing to this, this…ridiculous plan!"

I blushed, and Abby immediately sensed my discomfort, jumping in to add, "Ruth's desire to look in the eyes of the criminal who wronged her family is not ridiculous."

"Oh, I'm sorry, Ruth. I meant no offense," Mrs. Granville said to me, her eyes wide with embarrassment. "I can understand your desire to see and talk to Mr. Crane. But surely…oh, I just wish there was another way." She got up from the table and paced to the sideboard where she looked at that morning's breakfast offerings before taking nothing and reseating herself.

"Mother, there is no other way. Through no fault of our own—or Ted's—we've been given this opportunity to revisit a painful occurrence in our family's pasts. I think we should look at it that way—as a chance to right a wrong."

"Oh, Abigail, what on earth do you mean?" Mrs. Granville said, anguish and frustration causing her voice to quaver.

"When I first encountered Ted, I had no idea who he was and he didn't know me. It was only after we swapped histories that we found this common link among us, and just at a time when Ruth here was visiting, yet another person involved in this play. It would seem to me we were squandering an opportunity if we didn't go see Mr. Crane. It would seem as if we were…ungrateful…for not taking advantage of this chance that was dropped into our very laps."

Put that way, it did seem like a gift—to have run into Ted, just at the time he was here to work on his grandfather's case, and when I was here, a representative of the family most wronged, among us, by that man. But what kind of gift, I wondered. What was I supposed to do with this gift?

"Ungrateful? You seem to have no problem in turning your back on the gift of going to see one of the world's greatest tenors."

"Mother, I know you'll find suitable guests to accompany you. And you can tell us all about it after we return. Surely our mission is more important than listening to a man sing, no matter how well he does it."

"Ted's letter says he opposes this, too," Mrs. Granville said. "And I can understand why, Ruth. It hasn't escaped my attention that he has feelings for you. Naturally, he wouldn't want the woman he…a woman he's begun to feel affection for…to be exposed to something like San Quentin prison. It makes me think more highly of him that he's in agreement with me on this score."

Abby snorted and giggled. "Mother, listen to your talk! Being exposed to something like San Quentin prison—why, you'd think we wanted to run off and join the circus! It's just a building—"

"Where dangerous men are jailed!"

"Precisely. Jailed. Unable to get free. I suspect one is very limited in access to the more interesting parts of the prison."

"Oh, no, Abby, you can't be thinking of…" Mrs. Granville sighed heavily, but I could tell her glumness was receding. "Of course you're thinking of scouting around, aren't you? For a story? Sometimes I rue the day I let you take that job."

"Mother, you know by now it isn't a matter of letting me do anything."

"No, it isn't. It's more a matter of holding my breath, waiting to know you're safe after your latest escapade."

"There have been more?" I asked, sincerely curious, wanting to hear these tales.

At my clear eagerness to listen to Abby's stories, Mrs. Granville laughed, a good sound after so much tension.

"You have put me in a terrible position," Mrs. Granville said in a more serious tone. "If I refuse to give my permission to let you go, then Ted won't allow you to accompany him, and you will still probably go anyway."

Abby nodded slowly.

"If I say yes to this plan, then at least you have a strong young man accompanying you, and you're not going off wild and unprotected."

"I can take Papa's rifle," Abby said, as if just remembering it.

"I shudder at the thought of you with that firearm," Mrs. Granville said.

"I'm a good shot, Mother. That one time was an accident—"

"There is a third option," I interrupted quietly. They both stopped talking. I looked from one to the other. "You neither endorse nor oppose the plan. And that's how you really feel, isn't it? You don't want to encourage Abigail—and me—but you don't want to stand outright in our way?"

"Ruth, you've captured it," Mrs. Granville agreed.

"Then simply say nothing. Ted would not let us accompany him if he knew you opposed the trip. While he'd obviously prefer to have your permission, he would probably accept your lack of opposition as an alternative."

"I'd make sure he would," Abby interjected. She looked at her mother, reaching over to give her hand a squeeze. "I promise you, Mother. We'll be careful and not foolish. We'll be back straightaway, as soon as our visit is over. And I'll make sure Ruth is taken care of."

Mrs. Granville frowned and sighed but ultimately nodded. "I can't endorse this plan—" she looked at me "—I certainly couldn't justify it to your parents, Ruth. But I know my opposition will do nothing but imperil you since you'd go off on your own, without Ted, and he will only escort you with my blessing."

"Or, as Ruth said, at least without your opposition," Abby added, smiling at me.

Mrs. Granville looked up. "You may tell Ted I will not oppose the plan."

THE PLAN—WOULD THAT we had one! Abby and I hurried through the rest of breakfast, eager to get in touch with Ted. It took us an entire day, as he was out and about on legal business for his grandfather. So it wasn't until the next morning—a Sunday—that we were able to let him know we'd be accompanying him on Tuesday.

We shared this news at the church lemonade gathering after services, and he pressed Mrs. Granville on whether she was comfortable with the plan.

"I don't think I would say 'comfortable,'" she began before Abby interrupted with, "she'll not oppose it, and that's all I think we can ask of her."

In the excitement to plot out the visit, I'd almost forgotten that I'd written my mother telling her I'd be traveling home on Wednesday so I could take advantage of the tickets to the opera Mrs. Granville was generously providing Tuesday night—an event we wouldn't be able to attend now. Oh, well, visiting Mr. Crane would surely yield as good a harvest of comfort and enlightenment as the great tenor's singing. And I'd not lied when I'd told my mother of that plan, not yet knowing this new one.

I voiced these concerns to Abby and Ted. "I told my mother I was delaying my return in order to hear Mr. Caruso sing," I confessed.

"Don't fret about that," Abby said, touching my arm. "The earliest you could get a train is tomorrow anyway. It's just two days later."

She turned to Ted. "Should we be prepared to leave tomorrow?" she asked him. The prison was a good thirty miles away—an all-day journey by horse, plus a ferry ride over the bay. We'd have to pack bags for an overnight stay to be there for Ted's visit on Tuesday morning.

Ted paused, twisting his mouth to one side as he thought. "No," he said at last. "We'll set out very early Tuesday morning. Can you be prepared by dawn?"

"Of course!" Abby said.

Then he looked at me, trouble clouding his eyes. "You're planning on leaving this week?" he said in a near-whisper.

I looked down. "I have to get home some time. They'll worry. I—I've still not bought the ticket."

WHILE IT WAS STILL dark on Tuesday, Abby knocked softly at my door to rouse me, and we both attended to our morning preparations before padding downstairs for some coffee and bread. Mrs. Granville shared breakfast with us, still dressed in her robe, her hair flowing down her back. She was a striking woman, more so without all the "fixing" required for society. She must have still been worried about us because she hardly said a word, only that she'd like to speak to Ted alone when he arrived. We ate hurriedly and ran back upstairs to finish getting ready.

By the time we were done with these preparations, the doorbell rang. Ted had arrived.

And what an arrival!

"Ladies," he said as Abby and I came to the foyer, "I am pleased to inform you that an overnight stay might not be necessary."

Mrs. Granville joined us, now dressed, her hair neatly combed, as usual, into a full bun at the nape of her neck. At this news, she brightened. "No need for a stay?"

Seeing her relieved look, he quickly changed his tone, nervously fingering his hat before him. "I'm sorry, Mrs. Granville. I should have said that the outing might be shorter than anticipated, but we'll—I—still need to go. It's just, we can return this evening."

"How on earth—" Abby started to ask, but Ted had reopened the door and gestured to the street. There sat an automobile, the first rays of dawn glinting from its dark metal hood.

"This Ford F can go as fast as thirty miles an hour, I'm told, but with traffic and poor roads, it might take us several hours to reach San—" he looked at Mrs. Granville "—our destination."

We all stepped out to admire the car. I'd seen horseless carriages before, of course. Here in the city, they were common sights along with the horse-drawn wagons and cable cars. Even in the valley, one of the more "modern" ranches had bought one. Father always teased its owner about how often the car needed a repair of some sort. But I myself had never ridden in one. Would it be as frightening as my first trolley ride? Thirty miles an hour—how frightening that would feel, just sitting there, with no control over the movement. Not like being on a horse or in a carriage with people who knew horses…

I laughed inwardly. Here I was, a girl of fierce courage, or so I'd thought, frightened of a mechanical contraption! I wasn't afraid of the train, why should I fear this? I was glad my brother wasn't around to mock me.

"You know how to drive this?" Mrs. Granville asked, looking it over.

"As a matter of fact, I do. I drove a little back in New York, and one day I intend to own one of these fine machines." Ted stepped to the front of the car. "You first crank it and then—"

"Oh, don't explain it to me now," Abby exclaimed, coming forward to admire it. "I want to hear every step of the process when you're driving. Can I try?"

"Abby! You may not try driving. Really!" Mrs. Granville shook her head in amazement. She didn't seem bothered by the prospect of the automobile trip, however, which was reassuring.

"But how will you cross the bay?" she asked Ted.

"The ferry Ukiah accommodates automobiles," he said. "And since we don't need to adhere to the train schedule, we can set our own pace and hurry back when we're done."

Now that those worries were receding, another entered my mind—how had Ted been able to afford this?

"Is it yours?" I asked, almost to myself. I was lost in thought.

But Ted heard me. "No. I am borrowing it for the day—from a gentleman who can use the money more than the vehicle. If I like it, I might buy it from him."

Buy it! How expensive that would be! I had to bite my tongue to keep myself from asking that very question.

"Well, ladies, we should start off if we're to come home before the opera. No need to cancel that plan now. Our early start will give us several hours at our destination, which should be sufficient time to accomplish our tasks. But we can't be late for the first ferry."

Abby and I hurried inside to prepare. I suggested we lay out our opera clothing, in case we needed to change quickly when we returned, and Abby was grateful for the idea. I had to help her find a suitable garment, one appropriate for such a grand occasion and one not stained or ripped or frayed or otherwise in a state of disrepair. She instructed the housekeeper to air the dresses while we gathered our things—she insisted we take a small valise into which we both crammed overnight items, just in case we wouldn't be back in time and had to stay overnight, and she added to the housekeeper's tasks by asking her if she'd pack us some luncheon items. After all this, we finally rushed back outside. As we headed toward the slightly open door, I overheard the end of a conversation, the private one Mrs. Granville had insisted on having with Ted.

"…and I don't mind you asking. It's only natural you'd wonder. As you can well imagine, it's a source of shame for me, and I don't like to volunteer it." Ted's voice.

"You should go to the authorities, Ted. Set things right…."

"It will do little good now, Mrs. Granville. It won't help…." At that, he must have noticed the door opening, and he stopped, turning his attention to us instead. He smiled and rushed to aid us with our bags. With his hand on my elbow, he helped me into the front seat beside the wheel. Abby settled into the back seat on her own. He handed us both light blankets, telling us we could use them over our laps in case a spring chill was too bracing at our "breakneck" speeds.

With that, our adventure began. He cranked the car and managed to get it going—after a few starts that sputtered into nothing. While he worked on getting the engine rumbling, Mrs. Granville, upon his instructions, fetched us scarves to tie around our hats so that they'd not be blown off.

Within a few minutes, we were riding down the road with Ted chattering away about the vehicle's inner workings.

To my surprise and delight, I thoroughly enjoyed the ride. Unlike with the cable car, I didn't feel out of control with this drive. Having the driver sitting next to me, trusting him and his abilities, helped a great deal. Besides, despite the claim that the car could get up to thirty miles an hour, we didn't seem to go much over half that, often far slower as Ted maneuvered around holes and other traffic. My most serious moments of trepidation came when Ted had to maneuver the auto onto the ferry. But he instructed us to get off and walk on while he drove the machine into the big gaping space, and the one-hour crossing felt luxurious, like a holiday cruise, with the smell of salt water and brisk air to cheer us. Abby was a fountain of words, exclaiming about this sight or that person, and it was hard not to chuckle continuously at her happy jabbering.

By the time we hit more open road heading north on the other side of the bay, we were all completely relaxed. It felt more like a picnic outing than a visit to a penitentiary. The sun was shining, the air was mild and clean, and our spirits were high.

We stopped to have a midmorning snack near a beautiful meadow filled with wildflowers and butterflies, the occasional cawing or chirping bird providing music.

It was nearly impossible not to feel lighthearted in this atmosphere, but two thoughts tugged at my heart, coloring it with shadow as we moved forward.

I kept thinking of what Ted had been saying to Mrs. Granville before we left, about feeling shame and not going to the authorities. Did this have to do with his obvious newfound wealth? I remembered how we'd urged him to go to the police about possible gang hideaways. Was that what he was talking about—he'd not done it? And why not?

And the other shadow—why, it loomed ahead of us soon enough. The gray, unforgiving walls of San Quentin.

Chapter Fifteen

SILENCE FELL OVER us all as we approached it. Situated on a piece of land jutting into San Francisco Bay, it could have been an idyllic resort if not for the obvious signs that its visitors were not allowed to roam free—a two-story guardhouse sheltered armed men watching the environs, and beyond this the prison itself was drab and unfriendly-looking, as if daring anyone to approach.

Abby immediately pulled out her notebook, ready to record her observations of the place, while Ted left the car idling to deal with the guard, telling him why we were there and who we were to visit.

After parking the car, Ted helped us down, and we began walking to a far door. On the way, he talked but didn't look at us, instructing us on how we were to proceed. He was clearly uneasy, and my heart went out to him. We'd burdened him by insisting on coming with him. These trips were probably already difficult enough for him.

"We will meet my grandfather in a visitor's room. He will be shackled, so there is no cause for alarm. All prisoners with visitors are shackled. Three of us cannot go in at once—"

"I'll wait outside," Abby immediately volunteered. "My mission isn't the same as yours."

"There's a place where you can wait," Ted explained. "I also need to speak with a warden. My purpose today is to make sure Grandfather receives the medical care he needs. The prison has not acted with alacrity on this request, and if he has not yet been seen by a doctor, I am going to threaten legal consequences, although I'm not precisely sure what those will be."

"I could write a story about it," Abby said. "With your permission, of course!"

Ted smiled but didn't say anything.

Soon we were inside, and I was struck by how cold and damp it felt and smelled. In the distance, one could hear some sounds, men talking, a shout here and there, the occasional clank of a metal door.

After Ted spoke to yet another guard, handing him what must have been a certificate attesting to our permission to visit, he instructed Abby to wait in the lobby while we were ushered into a nearby room with several tables, chairs on either side of them. A few prisoners sat at them talking to their visitors, their hands and ankles contained with chains, their faces dirty and unshaven. They were dressed in striped uniforms. Guards stood at the two doors to the room—one door had bars at its window.

"They'll bring him to us," Ted said, gesturing me to an empty table. I noticed his hand shook a little. He was nervous.

My heart pounded, too. Here was my opportunity to face my grandparents' tormentor so many years ago. Did I have a right to do this? Who was I to judge him? Maybe this had been a foolish idea, after all. So many ideas seem good in thought and become foolhardy in action. Foolhardy and painful. I blushed with shame thinking of how Abby and I had so lightly and thoughtlessly underestimated the difficulties Ted faced when coming to this place. We'd treated it as lark, in a way, when it was a deeply disturbing necessity for Ted.

The far door clanked open, and a guard escorted a haggard man to our table. I'd thought perhaps I'd recognize him in some instinctual way, that some part of myself would know it was Billy Crane without being told, even though I'd never set eyes on him before. But there was no spark of recognition in my heart, only the sad observation of a clearly ailing old man, bent by age and racked by the ravages of a poorly chosen life. He had a gaunt face, his cheeks sunken and covered with a stubbly black-and-gray beard. His stringy white hair was combed off his face and in need of a cutting. The collar of his shirt was dirty, and he coughed a great deal before sitting down. This caused Ted to immediately start questioning him.

"Have you seen a doctor yet?"

"No." He coughed again, turning his face away from us as his body was racked by spasms.

Ted looked away and grimaced. "You were supposed to be seen by one by now."

After his grandfather stopped coughing, he turned back to face us, and Ted realized he'd not introduced us. As he did so, Mr. Crane stared, unblinking, into my eyes. I didn't flinch. I had my own scouring gaze locked on him, searching, searching…

"You don't look like her at all. Not 't all," he said in a low voice filled with awe and pain. This short declaration led to another cough, so rumbling from his chest and sore to hear that I feared he would collapse before me. He turned away and waved his chained hands at me, as if to apologize or perhaps to urge me to leave. But I stayed put.

Ted, however, was approached by a guard, who whispered something in his ear. Frowning, he turned to me and his grandfather. "The warden can see me now. I'd asked for a meeting over your health situation, Grandfather."

"You shouldn't bother," Mr. Crane said.

I saw Ted's shoulders slump at the implication—a man slated for execution needn't be healthy on the gallows. "It's important. To me, if not to you." He looked at me.

"I'll send Abby in while I attend to this," he said.

I nodded. I suspected he'd find Abby missing from the lobby, off "reporting" on whatever she saw. I didn't care. I actually looked forward to the time alone with Mr. Crane, if you could call being in a room with a dozen other folks "alone."

After Ted left, Mr. Crane had one more coughing jag.

When he was in control of himself, his face was as pale and ashen as the gray of his clothing and the dirty silver of his hair. His eyes were dark, of fathomless color, but rimmed with something that signified a wounded spirit, grateful for any crumb of mercy a kind soul would provide. At that point, I wasn't sure if I was up to that task. It wasn't that forgiveness wasn't part of my nature, but rather, that it wasn't mine to give. He hadn't wronged me except as an echo of what he'd done to my grandparents years ago. The forgiveness he sought was not mine to bestow.

"I'm sorry," he said. I thought he meant for the coughing fit and was about to suggest he need not apologize for that which he could not control, when he went on: "I should not have mentioned your grandmother. I have no right to speak of her, having caused her and your grandfather considerable worry and suffering."

My mouth, hanging open with my previously unvoiced assumptions, closed shut. I didn't know what to say. And again, he bridged my uncertainty by speaking with deliberate honesty.

"I have had ample time to reflect on that part of my life," he said with a matter-of-fact remorse that dared anyone to judge him insincere, "and I think I was jealous of your grandmother and Daniel—your grandfather. I think I believed I'd never have what they had. And then I went about setting up a life that made sure I'd not be disappointed in that creed."

"I...I'm glad you brought this up," I said, now feeling silly and small in the face of such a canyon of suffering. I crossed my gloved hands in front of me on the table and pulled from some inner well the courage I needed to fulfill my mission.

"No need to explain. I imagine you need to figure out for yourself if I'm telling you the truth about my remorse. I wish I could put your mind at ease on that score. But I reckon no amount of jawing with me is going to satisfy— are they still alive, your grandparents, both of 'em?" His tone was so eager, as if he were afraid they had passed before he'd had a chance to offer apologies to them. Ted must not have shared anything more than he needed to about my family. This was reassuring.

"Yes," I breathed.

He nodded. "Your grandmother was a beauty. I think I was in love with her. That's if I even knew what love was back then. Yes, I think I was jealous mostly of Daniel, for having so much love rained on him when I felt like a motherless child. It pains me terrible to think of all the people I've hurt. Why, Ted there, his grandmother, well, I didn't even try very hard with her, not really. Not after being swept off my feet and all. I thought that would see me through. But love's first blush ain't enough to keep a drifting man tethered. No, you've got to have the goodness deep down in your soul for that, anchoring you, or you at least got to want it real bad. And that goodness was still something I'd pushed away, just the way I pushed her away—dear, dear Beth…" His voice cracked, and he sniffled and sucked in his lips, overcome. "Never had a chance to say—" Again, he stopped, overwrought.

After a few seconds to regain control, he looked up and stared into my eyes. "Know this—whatever hardships I suffered, they played no role in my deeds. I alone was responsible for my misdoings. I alone committed the sin, not those whose loss I mourned, not those who'd wronged me in the past."

What a tortured soul he was, at a time of his life when people—such as my grandparents—looked back over full years populated by loved ones, by sorrows and joys, but by uplifting life, by grace. Yet here he was, tormented by all he'd done wrong, by all those he'd pushed out of his life, that he'd harmed, unable to rest knowing he'd hurt many and could not pay adequate restitution before his days were over.

It now seemed cruel to sit before him and search for sincerity. I felt I should be apologizing.

"I imagine you wondered, when you saw my note—Ted said he'd give it to you—how heartfelt it might be," he said, returning to his earlier thoughts.

"I must admit I did." That was why I sat before him now.

"As I say, I can't give you any evidence, nothing to hold in your hand, nothing to take back to those good folks, that will prove once and for all that I'm a changed man. But if it helps you any, it's the least I can do to share my tale…

"For many a year I led a sinful life, too awful for your delicate ears to hear about. Except for a pause when I married Ted's grandmother, I was a free and rowdy man, not caring who got in my way when pleasure was on my mind. And one night, after a four-night spree that had my vision as cloudy as a windstorm and my nerves as frayed as lightning, I nearly got myself killed by laughing at a mean ole cuss in a saloon. I don't even remember why I laughed, but when I did, he pulled out his gun and would have shot me through the heart except for the quick action of a stranger, who managed to bump into the gunman, causing his aim to go wild into the wall. After that, a few good folks wrestled him to the floor, and I got away clean. But not really, 'cause for days after I wanted to be able to thank that soul. I even went back to the bartender, asking about him, asking how I could find the fellow. And that barkeep, he just said he didn't know the man, but he suspected the best way I could thank him was to lead a good life, one worthy of being saved.

"That stuck with me. Leading a life worthy of being saved. And I tried to, from that moment on. Not always succeeding. But I tried. A stranger had saved my life. Surely I could save myself. It seemed mighty simple after that."

"Just as Ted's trying to save it now."

He smiled at the mention of his grandson. "He's a good boy, Theodore is. He's tryin' mighty hard."

"He believes in your innocence," I said, almost defensively.

"Why, that, he does," Mr. Crane concurred. "And don't fret. He's not wrong to do so. I didn't commit *that* crime."

"You think you deserve your...sentence...even though you're not guilty?" I asked, burrowing for more truths.

He sighed. "There's a peace in it," he said simply. "Knowing you're paying somehow for all you done wrong. Hard as it is, there's a peace in it. But I don't want to burden nobody now. And I know if it should come out how I was not guilty after the hangin' is done, some poor fellow here will have it on his soul that he led an innocent man to the noose. That doesn't sit lightly with me, Miss Ruth. And it's the only reason I've let Theodore help me."

So, but for the guilt it would hoist on another man, Billy Crane was willing to accept his execution with no protest.

Who can judge a man in one sitting? I didn't know if I could, but I knew I had enough to report to my parents and grandparents to lighten their hearts of concern about Ted's quest. As hard as this task was, it was lifting the burden of worry from my heart. Now I knew I could argue with my parents should they object to a friendship with Ted. His grandfather had exhibited sincere remorse in my presence, not a single drop more than he could demonstrate, not showy pretense, just forthright regret.

"Mr. Crane," I said, "it would help Ted considerably if you could recall anything more about this witness...this preacher you said you saw...." Maybe I'd uncover some detail Ted hadn't been able to find. That would make this visit doubly beneficial.

"Yes, ma'am." He folded his hands in front of him.

"You have described him as having a small scar like a half moon on his upper lip, of being slight in frame, of having white hair. Is there anything else you remember?"

"That's right. I told Theodore all that."

I noticed he didn't call his grandson "Ted." Was that Ted's request or his grandfather's distance?

He went on: "He kept pressing me for more details, too, but I can't seem to recollect any."

"What about what he told you, how he spoke? Did he mention anyone, did he talk of a place where he came from?"

After closing his eyes for a few moments, he spoke slowly. "He seemed to come out of nowhere. I'd ridden into the wild to clear my mind after I'd nearly decked a man because he'd insulted me in a bar. A saloon—I shouldn't have been within a mile of one, but there I was that afternoon. At least the fight—or prospect of it—kept my hand away from whiskey. This gentleman, he knocked into me, spilling the brew, and I pulled myself up, ready to set him to rights with a quick punch. But just as I stared him down, the barkeep came over and handed me another drink. I'd not ordered one—what was this? Then he apologized and gave it to the other fellow. Looking at him gulp it as if he'd been dreaming of drink for months on end, I realized he and I did look alike— same build, same color hair, similar clothes. The barkeep was to be forgiven for his confusion. As for me, it was as if I were staring at my future self—or more rightly, my past one since I'd been sober for more than, oh, ten years before this lapse—here was a man beaten down and worn, with an edge to his stare and a clumsiness about his general presence, so clumsy that even in a near empty saloon he rocks into me. But maybe, I reckoned, he'd done that intentionally just so as he could prove other people existed, that he wasn't alone.

"It both disgusted and humbled me. Sick at heart, I left the bar, grateful for the encounter that kept me from one sip of the poison that had helped me damage my own life. I didn't know where to go. I'd lost a job that morning, you see, not because of any action on my part but because the store owner couldn't afford to keep me on when a young brother of his, who'd just married and was going to be starting a family, needed work.

"My brother, of course, had long since been gone, but this small reminder of how fortunate are those whose older siblings look out for them and keep them safe, it set me simmering. I had none, mine having been stolen from me long ago—to my credit, ma'am, I did not then nor after think on the incident of my brother Pete's drownin' as the fault of your grandfather, as I once had done. No, I just looked on it as general misfortune now. But that didn't stop me from bemoaning my sorry fate and all the stupid decisions I'd made in life since Pete's passing that had led me to sorrow more often than not.

"I rode away feeling an awful sense of regret and, oddly enough, gratitude. Had I not just been saved from drink? And this made me realize the many times I had been saved from something, from the stupidity of my own decisions, from that of others. I guess you could say that I counted my blessings for the first time in my life, and it was a sweet moment to feel, at last, a sense that I'd not mucked up my life so bad that I couldn't recognize the times I'd had it good, or at least had been spared something bad. It was fearsome.

"All this thinking took place as I wandered out of town aimlessly, and I finally decided to set up camp—lay myself down really—for the night near a rocky formation northeast of town, a place I knew from my original drive into San Francisco, oh, those many years ago.

"It felt peaceful, like coming home." He paused to clear his throat, but this led to another coughing fit that left him so red-faced and gasping I feared not hearing the rest of his tale. As if realizing his time might be measured in increments smaller than days, he hurried on:

"In the morning, my peace was broken. I'd foolishly left my fire untended—it was the first real sleep I'd had in years—and I was dismayed to see my horse had wandered off. I couldn't fault her. She was a new mare, bought with my last month's wages. I dusted myself off and went in search of her, finding her before the noonday sun had risen and realizing during my wandering that this time for reflection was good for me, good for what ailed me. I decided to treat it as such, a retreat into the desert, just as our Lord had done—don't be thinking I'm comparin' myself to him none, though; I know my place as a recent sinner.

"There in the distance, in the wavy midday air, was Jezebel—that was the horse's name when I bought her— being patted by this man, nuzzling at his face as he talked to her. When he looked at me, it was as if he'd been expecting me. He waved me on over with such kindness that I left suspicion behind.

"He told me he was calming Jezzy since a rattlesnake had slithered on by. 'Jezzy,' I blurted. How'd he know her name? He laughed and said he knew mine, too— William—that he'd been watching me. Where, I put to him, in the city? He nodded and said 'thereabouts.' And then he told me he'd come into the countryside to pray, that it was the only thing that cured his 'rattlin' nerves' sometimes, and he hadn't yet done his morning talk with the Almighty and did I mind if he did so now since he was feeling a mite fretful of putting it off.

"Of course I didn't mind, but I was sure surprised when he slipped to his knees with no delay, as if someone had pushed him to the ground. I'd expected him to go off somewhere or at least to just offer a silent conversation and decided to do my own, but he commenced to talking as if God were standing right in front of him and they was havin' the friendliest of talks.

"'Cept it weren't no friendly chatter like I'd ever heard. It was like music, filled with fine-sounding words and phrases, and all from the heart, too, not like some slicked-up salesman trying to oil you up with flattery so you'll be giving him your treasure.

"He started out with lots of praise and thanksgiving—I wish I could remember how he said it, it was a beautiful thing to hear, and it lifted my soul up along with his, making me feel like I was the one offering all those pretty words and thoughts.

"And then he moved on to asking for help for people he knew, sometimes telling the Almighty, just as if He were a friend he'd known a long time, all the little ins and outs of the things people needed. Like a new rifle. He asked that somebody name Rengles be able to get a new rifle, not for 'shootin' up the town or causing no end of trouble but so's he can go hunting with his son and help him put food on the table and gain his pride back after losing something important. The man even prayed for me, though we'd just met. He asked God to help his 'new friend find what he's looking for,' as if he knew I was out here looking for something, some peace I'd never felt much in all my years.

"And then he ended by asking for forgiveness for his sins, even naming a few which sounded to me like nothing more than the little mistakes we make every day, nothing more meaningful or bad than forgetting to say thanks to somebody or not visiting a sick friend 'cause of feeling sick hisself. Shoot, I could have given him a list worth mentioning. Anyways, at the end he asked to help him stay on the 'path to righteousness.' And he got up."

"But didn't you ask him where he came from?" I asked, exasperated. Hearing the story made it seem even more incredible still.

"Why, of course I did, ma'am. And he just said no place in particular, just here and there, wherever he felt called to help."

"Didn't you ask how he knew you, how he knew your horse's name?" I inquired, my frustration coming through in my pinched voice. I modulated my tone. Sounding accusatory would not help me dislodge any new memories…or uncover the real truth should he be dissembling. "Surely you had more conversation with him out there in the wilderness."

He smiled and nodded before coughing again, though this time his discomfort was brief. "Yes, we talked. We talked about the Almighty, about why we were both far from home, about what a soul needs when everything in the world seems parched and dry."

"But nothing about—"

"About the small items in our daily lives, whether we like sugar in our coffee, or don't care much for the summer sun? No, Miss Ruth, I'm afraid not. I know this story sounds as tall as an ancient redwood, but I can only tell it like it happened. I went wandering sore in spirit, I found a man who offered me respite, I accepted the grace he had to give and did not let the particulars of our meeting—and their lack of details—mar the experience. Practicalities seemed rather trivial at the moment, almost…a betrayal of the gift he gave me."

"Gift? He gave you something?"

He shook his head, his smile leaving him. "No, he gave me nothing but his good will and companionship. We both rode back into town after that encounter—he had his horse tied up nearby—and once we were at the city's edge, we parted ways."

"Which way—which way did he go?" Now, at last, we were getting somewhere. I was surprised Ted hadn't asked that question.

But he had. "As I told my grandson, the preacher man headed toward the harbor. That's the last I saw of him." The harbor. Jane Stillweather had said she'd seen such a man near the harbor. Maybe she wasn't as addled as others claimed.

"He seemed to know that area of town?" I asked.

"Yes. He seemed comfortable there, as if he knew it, come to think on it."

So it could have been where he'd stayed when he rested. Ted needed to search more in that area. We all did. Why hadn't any leads turned up there?

"He might have seen me there, heard my name, my horse's name," Mr. Crane mused. His eyebrows lifted with a new thought. "You know, I told Theodore he was a 'preacher man,' but he never said as much. And he didn't wear no collar or nothing else to suggest it. It was just the way he talked an all."

Maybe he wasn't a preacher at all! Maybe he was just an ordinary man, someone who worked at a stable or near one—that's how he might have known of Mr. Crane and his horse. Maybe he was merely an itinerant *worker*. By always asking if people had seen this preacher, we'd probably muddied the waters of their memories. Maybe he didn't minister at all, except in the purely personal sense. I could hardly wait to tell Ted.

"His wisdom stuck with me," he said, lost in thought. "Still lingers. It was powerful stuff."

He looked up at me. "I find myself turning things over in my mind, asking myself what that man might say about them. Like the money…I've thought a lot about that, whether I told Theodore the right thing to do."

"The money…" I said, my heart growing cold, afraid of what I was about to learn.

"I've told Theodore where I thought it might be. That old Crispin gang would do this kind of job—run in quick and overpower a homesteader or other sorry soul. They chose the weak and unprotected for their work, not the powerful. It's a mark of their depravity and desperation that they attacked this other rascally clan and did the killing—maybe they was angered at them. Another thing for me to offer thanks for—that I'd left that gang behind long ago. There's an old gold-mining outfit northeast of town, off a road that looks little more than a dirt track into the wilderness. My guess is it's there, waitin' for the time when the hangman's done his job. Theodore knows it. I drawed him a map."

That was the area Ted and I'd gone into. He'd been following his grandfather's directions. Had he found the stash? Was that the reason for his current comfortableness, the new clothes, the better housing?

"You see, I told Theodore he should find the money and keep it for hisself. It's profit from another bad gang—I know from the court reports. But now I'm feeling poorly for making that suggestion to Theodore. I shouldn't be encouraging him to do wrong things as if it would make other things right. That's the kind of bad thinking that put me on the path to perdition. Hard to shake off, after all. You tell him that, will you? I know he's got a good heart. But he's got a heavy burden taking care of his sister, and he might be tempted. Do tell him, will you? The Lord will provide…"

Before I could ask any more, the jailer came and told Mr. Crane his visiting time was over. The guard looked at me suspiciously since my male companion had not come back to accompany me, but I ignored his harsh stares. My heart was too vexed by now to worry about a stranger's opinion.

As Billy Crane stood, he looked at me and rasped out, "Do not be troubled, young lady. I am at peace. My days are numbered, no matter which ways they end."

And he was gone, leaving me in the dank-smelling room biting my lip and stifling tears.

DO NOT BE TROUBLED. How could I not be? I'd gone to San Quentin looking for truth, hoping to see for myself what kind of man Billy Crane was, whether my mother was right to warn me away from him for the family's sake.

And I came away from the visit more secure in his remorse and innocence, yes, but now deeply bothered by what he'd said about Ted. He'd told Ted to take the money for himself! Had this been Ted's goal all along—to get from his grandfather the information on where the loot was stored? At least that meant Ted really did believe his grandfather innocent...unless he thought his grandfather would tell him where he himself had secreted the money if he'd done the deed.

My head throbbing, I made my way back to the lobby. Abby had returned at least. She sat on a bench scribbling away in her notebook, only looking up when I stood before her.

"Oh...is Ted coming? Is it time to go already? How was your visit?" As if remembering our mission, she stood, the notebook and pencil dropping from her lap to the floor. "Oh, Ruth, did you find what you came for?"

I nodded, tears in my eyes. She immediately embraced me, but she didn't know the full meaning of my words or my sadness. I felt encased in ice, frozen in time, not able to move forward.

Just then, Ted appeared, sauntering toward us, a grim look on his face. As Abby collected her dropped items, he spoke.

"The warden assures me Grandfather will be seen by a physician, but I have no confidence it will be any time soon. Now I've missed an opportunity to talk with him, too! And I had items to discuss."

He looked at me. "I hope your meeting wasn't too difficult," he said in a softer tone. "Did you feel satisfied that he was sincere?"

"Yes," I said. "Very much so." I probed his eyes with my gaze, wishing I could be equally sure of his sincerity and innocence. "He also told me some more about the 'preacher' we've been searching for. And about the gang that might have done the deed."

"Wonderful, Ruth! Great job. Tell us all," Abby said.

But Ted was already ushering us out the door to the car. "Regale us with the story on the way home. I promised your mother, Abby, that I'd have you both home in time for the opera, and I want to keep my word."

We hurried to the car, but it took Ted a good quarter hour to get the engine started. Then the noise from the motor made conversation difficult. I did manage to share my theory that we'd been wrong to see the missing witness as a preacher, that he was perhaps an ordinary laborer who happened to be loquacious about his faith. This perked up both Ted and Abby considerably and set them to talking about how to start a new search for him, leaving out the "preacher" part of the description. The motor noise was such, though, that they often ended up repeating questions and answers, or I was cast in the role of translator from front to back seat and back again.

In fact, this discussion spilled over into the ferry boat ride, with Abby excitedly suggesting new avenues of investigation, which she vowed to begin the very next day.

After those ideas were thoroughly discussed, I saw no point in holding back the rest of my conversation with Mr. Crane, and I mentioned, in as matter-of-fact a tone as I could manage, what he'd told me about the Crispin gang and their hideaways and how he'd wrestled with the advice he'd given Ted over taking the riches for himself. By this time, however, we were on terra firma again, back in the car. Perhaps it was better this way, I reasoned, making this tricky part of discussion more "casual," less pointed.

Ted nodded glumly at my recitation. "That's true. He told me that."

"Oh, dear," Abby interjected, leaning forward from the back seat, her hand holding her hat on—she'd neglected to tie a scarf around it.

"I wish he hadn't said anything to you," he said to me, keeping his eyes on the road. It seemed to me he was driving faster home than on the way to the prison. Was he trying to outrun his conscience?

"Did you ever go to the police about those possible hiding spots?" I asked Ted.

"No, I did not," he said, sounding a little snappish. "I'm not convinced finding them would help prove my grandfather's innocence."

I looked at him, dapper and fresh in his new suit, the edge of the gold watch glinting from its pocket. Was there another reason he'd not gone to the police? Could it be because, to his shame, he *had* followed his grandfather's advice and found the treasure, keeping it for himself? I swallowed hard. How could I ask him that, without cruelly accusing him of the same kind of thievery his grandfather engaged in?

"So you ignored everyone's advice?" I asked as gently as I could.

But Ted understood my deeper meaning. "Yes, Ruth. Everyone's. Do you think I took whatever riches might be hidden in the hills? If there are any there?" He sounded wounded.

I couldn't answer. Not with Abby in the back seat. How could I accuse him further in front of her? It required a private conversation, and I now feared it would end badly, with no information discovered and only resentment stirred up.

We rode the rest of the way from the ferry in silence, Abby nodding off into a doze, I lost in my thoughts and Ted in his. Whatever Ted had said, I still couldn't reconcile his words with his situation. His grandfather had urged him to collect the money from the robbery. Ted knew where it might be. And he'd not gone to the police to report the possible hideaway. Then there were his improved circumstances to consider. A man so poor he could barely afford a cup of coffee now was dressed well and even thinking of buying a new automobile for himself. How could this be?

At last, as we neared the Granville home, I found my voice. I had to know more. The uncertainty was torturing me. I'd laid to rest as best I could my doubts about his grandfather. I had to do the same with Ted if I were to plead for his friendship with my family. "You seem to be doing better for yourself these days," I murmured, trying not to sound accusatory.

"Yes, I am," he said. "I'll be before a judge soon with my grandfather's case. I must look decent for that presentation."

"Of course you do. I didn't mean it as a criticism."

He turned to me as he pulled the car up in front of the Granville residence. "What did you mean?"

I looked into his eyes, afraid to ask but afraid not to. I had to find the same courage I'd used while talking to his grandfather. Honesty was no insult, Abby was fond of saying. Honesty, despite its wounding capacity, was what I'd have to count on. "Did the money...did it come from..."

"From ill-gotten means?" he asked, not looking at me. "Ruth, I—" He stopped, looked down, swallowed. Still without gazing at me, he continued, "I'm not proud of how it came to me. But I have to live and my sister has to live, and I must provide for us both. It's difficult for me to talk about."

With that, he accompanied us and a just-roused Abby to the door, squeezing my hand gently before bidding us farewell, saying he'd come round for us in a few hours' time for the opera.

Chapter Sixteen

OH, MY HEAD ACHED from so many bothersome thoughts as I entered the Granville home that evening. Twilight's shadows painted the foyer a dusky blue as I removed my gloves and hat, ready to make my weary way to my room. It was past dinnertime, and I had no appetite for food anyway.

Abby, however, was ravenous and said she'd head to the kitchen to see what was left over from dinner.

"Stella left some trifle and other tidbits, if you're hungry," she called out.

"Thank you, but I couldn't eat a bite. My head is splitting, I'm afraid," I said from the stairs.

"Oh, dear. Let me get you some bicarbonate of soda," she said, coming back into the foyer, a piece of bread in her hands. "Does wonders really. Go on up, I'll be there in a moment. Mother's getting ready, apparently. I suppose that means she didn't worry too much about us!"

I smiled at her busy helpfulness. There'd be no avoiding her, and I shouldn't try.

Once in my room, I quickly changed into a loose dressing gown, happy to have the stays and clasps of my more formal costume off my sore body. I looked at the elegant evening gown of shimmering rose hues hanging on the armoire. I wanted to wear my riding clothes again. Not the fancy ones I'd brought with me but the rougher, ranch clothes I'd left behind. I wanted to go home. I'd dallied long enough. I couldn't do any more to help Ted or his grandfather, and I wasn't even sure I should. I was consumed with a bewildering array of feelings— profound sadness for his grandfather but weary concern for Ted. Had he chosen the wrong path, after all? It seemed he'd all but confessed to doing so before Abby woke up in the car and we came inside. Did I need more proof he'd strayed from goodness? If we'd talked more, would he have just tried to convince me of the rightness of the choice he'd made?

After knocking softly, Abby bustled into the room, a glass with milky water in her hand. I accepted it and swallowed the salty brew, thanking her.

"I hope you feel better by the time we have to go. Maybe this day was too much for you," Abby said.

At that I bristled. "I've worked longer days on the ranch," I countered and then smiled at myself. "But thank you for your concern. I'll be fine after I sit for a few moments."

After a pause, I said, "I'll miss you so much. You'll have to come visit me—both of you. I know my mother and grandparents would love to see your mother."

"Yes, we've talked of it. Mother would very much like to see your family again. You're still planning on leaving tomorrow? You'll be so tired!"

I looked down. I was too tired to offer false courtesies, so I brought my head up and stared her in the eyes. "I've stayed too long as it is. I really need to head home."

She reached over and patted my hand. "Oh, Ruth, you are troubled. Is that why you're still insisting on going tomorrow? Have you told Ted? He surely will be disappointed."

"I've not had a chance to mention it—my specific departure. I'll leave a note." I'd avoided telling him what train I was taking—I'd not even made the reservation. What held me back? At first, I'd thought it was because secretly I wanted to stay and would find a reason to extend my visit. But as the day had worn on, I knew it was because I was afraid he'd see my suspicions and wonder if my departure was a more lasting break. I hated facing that possibility, so I'd kept my intention to leave tomorrow for sure to myself. As it was, I'd been frank with my suspicions of how he'd come into the money, and it had ended unsatisfactorily, with no real resolution.

She pulled back. "A note? But you'll be seeing him tonight! And he does know you're going soon! Oh. I see. You've had a falling out, a lover's quarrel. Did you argue while I was asleep in the car?"

At this I frowned. "We've had no such thing. We are not...courting."

"Perhaps *you* aren't, but I think Ted is. Oh, Ruth, are you still mourning your fiancé? I hope I'm not speaking out of line, but perhaps it's time to put that sorrow away and embrace the blessings God sends you—"

"I will never put my mourning away!" Suddenly, fury and sadness warmed me. I'd never had to worry about Miguel's intentions, never had to wonder whether he was doing something wrong. I'd been mistaken to try to forget him, to embrace the possibility of new love. That path had betrayed me. I wouldn't allow Abby to convince me otherwise. She didn't know of what she spoke.

"I'm sorry," she said in a chastised tone. "I didn't mean to suggest that you'll ever forget your loss. Please forgive me. I can be rudely outspoken. Mother chides me for this all the time."

At this, I smiled. Yes, she did. I'd witnessed it, and it was a beautiful and loving interplay that I'd miss when returning to Carmel Valley.

"Speaking of your family," Abby said, "you had several notes from them today. They're on the tray downstairs. I can get them—"

As she started to rise, I stopped her by putting my hand on her arm. "Don't trouble yourself. My eyes are too tired to read tonight. I'll look at them in the morning." I knew what they'd say anyway—come home, stay away from Billy Crane. I intended to heed those warnings and calls tomorrow. I'd write them a note…and Ted one, as well.

"This visit has meant so much to me," I said and then choked up, unable to convey what this new friendship really had meant. "You've opened my eyes to a new world. Maybe one day, I'll come live in San Francisco."

"That would be grand, Ruth! I'm so happy to hear you say that." She kissed me lightly on the cheek and squeezed my hands, her dimples deeply set as she smiled. "I'll let you rest now. Everything will seem better in the morning. I'm sure of it. Before you depart, you must see Ted. I mean really talk to him. It's only polite, no matter what you feel for him."

I nodded, not sure I'd follow through on that request at all.

I RESTED FOR A few moments, and then Abby and I helped each other dress. She insisted on threading a deep red velvet ribbon through my hair, and despite her negligence of her own looks, she was quite good at attending to mine. While I wore a new gown of light rose layers of fabric that hugged my upper torso while flowing gently to my toes, she had put on a dark green satin that she said made her feel like a stalwart tree. I helped comb her hair into a neat bun, pinning a peacock feather ornament into its luscious masses. We both chose jewelry for each other—a beribboned brooch for her and a small gold cross for me—and she found a dark satiny wrap for herself while I grabbed a brightly embroidered shawl that had been my father's mother's. After tugging on long gloves, we descended the stairs together.

Ted and Mrs. Granville stood in the foyer waiting, and when Ted saw us, his gaze stayed locked on mine. My eyes couldn't leave him either. He'd donned a dark suit and white shirt and bowtie. In his hands was a brushed top hat.

"My, how lovely you girls look," Mrs. Granville said. "Ted was just telling me about your adventure today. I'm so relieved it worked out."

Ted opened his mouth and closed it, as if not sure what to say. Then, finally, he managed to murmur, "I'm a lucky gentleman to be accompanying such beauties to the opera tonight," his gaze still on me.

He'd retained the use of the car, so we stepped in and were on our way in a few moments.

Despite my fatigue, despite my worries about Ted's money, the evening provided an idyllic respite.

It was as if entering into a fairy tale. The opera house itself was a jewel box of gilt tiers, three layers of them, as if they were a concave wedding cake, surrounding the stage. When the music began and the curtain opened, I was transported into another world.

I'd never heard opera before. The only music we listened to on the ranch were hymn sings and guitar ballads. A couple times, Mother and Father had taken us into Monterey to hear a traveling band. But I'd never heard anything as grand as this—the waves of sound, the heart-rending melodies, the singing that seemed to soar to the rafters.

And the story of the besotted Don Jose and traitorous Carmen! I wanted to fling myself onto the stage in the final act, warning him to stay away from her, not to lose his life and his soul to this unworthy—if passionate—creature!

The entire experience was so beyond comprehension that Enrico Caruso's voice was but one piece of a larger magnificence. At the end of it, I felt drained and uplifted at the same time, and our talk, as it had been during the intermissions, focused exclusively on the performance and its wonders.

Oh, yes, Ted's strong arms guided me to our seats, his shoulders warmed mine as we sat side by side, his strong profile was cast in silhouette as the lights dimmed, and he even squeezed my hand in the dark during stirring passages, causing my heart to gallop.

But at the end of the night, I was still wondering: who was he? Was he the pure and innocent Jose who began the opera, or the tempted and corrupted man who ended it?

When he bid us goodnight, Abby and Mrs. Granville hurried into the house, leaving us alone on the steps in the cool night air, but not before Abby announced that I was leaving soon.

Ted took my hands in his, his eyes shining. "When are you leaving? You've made your travel plans? Were you going to tell me?"

I looked down, my throat dry and clogged. "Tomorrow. I should have mentioned it."

"Ruth! Why? Were you not going to say anything to me, to let me see you off?" He sounded more than distressed, his voice a harsh whisper. It was as if I'd physically hurt him.

"I—I was going to write a note...."

"A note! But I thought..." He stopped and swallowed. "I thought you were open to my request to court you. Have I done anything to offend you?"

Offend me—how did I know, and how could I ask without offending him? It was impossible! *What was I to say: are you a thief, Ted, like your grandfather?* I'd come as close as possible to asking that question at the end of our excursion today, and he'd said he didn't like to talk about the matter.

"I am very grateful you took me to see your grandfather today, Ted. I want to report on that meeting and give my parents and grandparents his apology," I managed to say. And I needed time to think, to figure out how to find out what I wanted to know, or if I even had a right to the information.

"So you feel compelled to hurry home and not linger?" he asked, hopefulness in his voice. He didn't want to think my hasty retreat was for any other reason.

"Yes."

He leaned toward me, and our foreheads touched while he gently stroked my fingers. Then he angled his face, and our lips met for a sweet kiss filled with affection. It warmed me and made my knees weak. I felt consumed with a longing I'd not known was possible.

"Is that the only reason, Ruth?" he whispered after we pulled apart, his hands still on mine. "I sense you're keeping something from me."

Oh, how I wanted to tell him, to ask him! I couldn't stand it any longer. I had to at least give him a chance to defend himself.

"Your grandfather told me he wanted you to take the stolen riches if you found them," I said, my voice shaking.

I felt him stiffen. "Yes. You mentioned that in the car. What is it you want to know, Ruth?"

"Did you? Did you find them? Is that why you've been able to afford…new things? Is it why you don't want to talk about how you've afforded them? If it is, please, tell me, Ted. Please. I'd rather you be honest about it." Every ounce of my being craved to hear the truth, even if it was painful.

"You think that of me?" he asked in hushed indignation, dropping my hands. "You think I stole?"

"I…I will be frank. I don't know what to think." Why wouldn't he just tell me how he'd come into money suddenly?

He reached out and pulled me to stand in the dim light spilling from the window where one of the Granvilles must have lit a kerosene lamp.

"Look into my eyes, Ruth, as you looked into my grandfather's earlier today. I swear to you that I did not find nor take any riches from the robbery my grandfather is falsely charged with. Does that satisfy you?"

It did—up to a point. And he knew why. He wouldn't tell me where the money had come from. Why wouldn't he? The thought filled me with profound sadness. Lying, even if it was lying by not admitting the truth outright, just made things worse. But he'd told me—he'd sworn to it—that he'd not taken any riches from the robbery. Shouldn't that be enough? Shouldn't I believe he wasn't lying?

A few streets over, we heard horses neighing at a nearby livery stable. "They're restless tonight," Ted said. "A carriage driver told me his horses were acting up."

"Sometimes, when the weather changes, that happens," I said, not wanting to break the connection with him, but wanting to move beyond the discussion of…money. But inside, I knew it was too late. I'd hurt him deeply with my accusation in the form of a question. And I was hurting, too, by his inability to be completely open with me.

"Ruth, my family…my family is not fit for good society," he began, then stopped himself and looked away, as if the subject were too painful. "Do you trust me, Ruth?" he pleaded, staring at me again.

I looked into his eyes. Yes, I did. But only if I knew the full truth. Was that real trust?

When I didn't answer right away, he swallowed and grimaced, as if stung afresh. He knew what my silence meant. He looked down.

"I…I…love you, Ruth," he whispered into the night air. "I'd hoped you'd returned my sentiments." With gleaming eyes, he kissed my hand and walked back to the automobile. Before he could see my tears, I fled into the house.

I HARDLY SLEPT at all that night, my heart and mind filled with a thousand thoughts, regrets overtaking hope, optimism sliding into despair as I considered all possibilities.

He'd said he loved me. My heart pounded at those words, aching to shout back to him: I think I love you, as well, Ted Beaumont, don't give up on me.

No, don't give up on me, even though I'd almost given up on you.

After hours of half sleeping, half dreaming, I rose before dawn stretching and yawning in the cool blue light before the eastern rays of the sun reached us. I leaned on the desk below the window, breathing deeply of the fresh air. It ignited in me a powerful desire to be home, to be breathing the perpetually fresh air of the ranch, to be helping my father, making amends with my mother, loving my grandparents, guiding my brother, seeing Anita and her family before they left. And writing to Ted, begging him to forgive me, to resume his suit for my hand. I shook my head sadly. What a headstrong girl I was! Headstrong and confused.

After quickly washing and changing, I sat at the desk to pen a note to the Granvilles, first one to Abby gushing with affection and gratitude and again a plea to have her visit me, then one to her mother, a more formal but no less heartfelt letter, expressing similar emotions. And then I wrote to Ted, telling him how sorry I was for doubting him, that I hoped he would look past my rude questions, that I only wished what was best for him, and that I dearly hoped he would come see me in Carmel Valley. I wanted to believe every word of trust I'd included in the letter. Maybe time would make trust grow along with love. As I folded the notes, I heard Stella stir below, starting the stove for breakfast, putting on coffee, sweeping the kitchen. It was nearly five o'clock now.

After packing my bags, I made my way downstairs, where I surprised the housekeeper.

"Coffee's almost ready, ma'am," she said, brushing flour off her apron. I saw bread dough on the table behind her. "I could fix you something else, too…."

"Thank you, just some bread with jam will be fine. I also need to get to the train station—would someone be available to take me?"

"Jimmy, the stable boy, can drive a wagon for you. He'll be showing up soon for his breakfast."

After thanking her, I sat at the large table in the dining room, pulling yesterday's unread notes from the pocket where I'd placed them.

As I suspected, the letters from my parents urged me to keep my distance from Billy Crane, but they were also full of details about the ranch—a new foal had arrived, our hens were laying eggs in abundance, a neighbor had broken a wrist in an accident but was on the mend, and— here was sad news for my brother—Sally had returned from San Francisco engaged to Ralph. Oh, the man who'd met us both when we'd arrived what seemed ages ago! Poor Joe. Now, more than ever, it seemed as if I needed to go home as quickly as possible.

Sucking my lips in, I read my grandmother's sweet note. She merely repeated information my mother had shared, but I suspected hers was a more covert method of urging caution. She'd know that I would think of her and her feelings when reading her missive. I patted a pocket of my dress where I'd secreted Mr. Crane's letter of apology.

Stella came in to serve me coffee and bread just as the clock in the foyer struck five.

I heard a door open and close upstairs. Abby or her mother would be down soon.

And in a few minutes, Mrs. Granville did appear, still wearing her morning coat of embroidered silk.

"I thought I heard you, Ruth," she said as the housekeeper brought her coffee in. "Why are you up so early? Your train isn't scheduled this early, is it?"

Suddenly, I was impatient for action. I wanted to share with someone—Mrs. Granville, Abby—the anguish in my heart.

"I wish…I wish I could stay, but I need to go home, I need…" I blurted out, and through tears I shared with her my heartache, my questions to Ted the evening before, how he'd answered me, how he'd professed his love for me, and how I wanted to tell him I felt the same, but I'd been foolish, squandering this opportunity with my doubts and fears…doubts I still had!...and that perhaps I was destined to live alone after Miguel…that I didn't deserve happiness with another man….

"Oh, Ruth," she said, pulling a chair near me and clasping my hands in her own. "You poor dear. You poor child. Oh, darling, I cannot answer the questions in your heart about Miguel. I can only say that God surely doesn't intend for you to live in sorrow your entire life, and if you found another young man worthy of your affection…" She stroked my hair as I sobbed, and was silent for some time. When I was finally calm, she raised my chin and stared into my eyes.

"I know the story of Ted's money, my dear. Like you, I wondered, and, yesterday, before you left for San Quentin, I talked to him about it. I couldn't, in good conscience, allow you and Abigail to accompany him when I had doubts in my heart about his new fortune. I know it was wrong of me to pry into such personal matters, and I think he only opened up to me to allow your trip with him to continue, calming my fears." She smiled a little. "I know Abby would remind me of my own words not to stray into others' private lives, but I felt responsible for you, and if I had any doubts, even the smallest ones, that the man to whom I was entrusting your well-being was less than forthright, I had an obligation to set those doubts to rest, even if it meant being less than kind in my judgments."

I looked at her, holding my breath waiting for her to continue.

"Even though it breaks a confidence," she said, "I think it serves the greater good to tell you, to put your mind at ease." She straightened and sighed. "He very honestly answered my questions about his new riches yesterday. It weighs on him terribly, and he hasn't wanted to speak about it because it embarrasses him, he told me. It's a hard burden to bear. He found out…well… He didn't want to take the money but felt he had to—to provide for his sister and to start a practice here, to defend his grandfather…"

She proceeded to tell me the story. Ted had thought his father died when he was young, leaving his mother a widow. But he'd received a letter from his New York solicitor recently informing him that Rowland Beaumont, III had just passed away, leaving him a tidy sum but not his entire estate, nor a large part of it. It was enough to provide a decent annual allowance, but it was more an amount to assuage guilt from beyond the grave than to provide fairly for his children. It turned out Ted's father had deserted his family, marrying another woman without divorcing Ted's mother. He'd acted shamefully, and Ted had hesitated to take the money once he'd learned the truth. His solicitor had urged him to sue the estate for more of what was "rightfully his," but he refused to do so, preferring instead to leave the painful memories behind. To make matters worse, Ted had also found out from his grandfather that he had sent money to his grandmother a few times over the years, ill-gotten money. And now Ted wondered if any of it had been used to fund his education.

"He was so ashamed of what he discovered. He'd told everyone his mother was widowed! He'd thought a family trust had paid for his education! Every foundation in his life seemed to be crumbling away. But he has to keep moving forward to help his grandfather," Mrs. Granville said. "I myself urged him to go to the authorities and pursue a suit if the money should come to him—his father left the bulk of the estate to a distant nephew since he had no children with his new 'bride'."

How awful I'd probably made him feel with my interrogation! What right had I to press him on such a personal issue! Poor Ted—that's why he'd talked about his family not being fit for good society. He hadn't been referring to his grandfather but to his father.

Again, I'd been selfish. I had to see him, talk to him. A note was not enough…I'd take a later train, but first, I had to find him, to explain, to apologize….

So restless was I to get going that my hand shook the coffee cup on the table as my fingers rested on its saucer, spilling the liquid onto the lace cloth before me. Oh, dear. I hoped Stella could remove the stain. I stood to summon her but found my position tenuous, as if I were lightheaded. Perhaps I needed to eat a bit of fruit or have a glass of water….

Then I realized—my hand had not shaken. The room was shaking, rattling as if a huge hand were rocking it back and forth.

Mrs. Granville just murmured, "Oh!"

I heard a rumble and assumed it was a large carriage going by. Perhaps that was the reason for the movement?

But it didn't fade into the distance. A noise like thunder cracked the still air of dawn. The house shook, as if it were a rag doll in the hand of a petulant child. Pieces of plaster fell from the ceiling. A scream was heard in the distance. The room continued to tremble, again and again, as if in a fit. A picture fell off the wall crashing into the sideboard. The housekeeper uttered a cry as something crashed in the kitchen. Mrs. Granville stood, struggling to stay on her feet as the room seemed to rise and fall on a tide.

Just then, Abby appeared in the doorway, her eyes wide and mouth agape as she held on to the jamb to steady herself. Glass tinkled and broke, the chandelier sounding like wind chimes in a gentle breeze. The clock in the parlor let out sonorous bongs at irregular fast-paced intervals. I held on to the chair and watched a porcelain knickknack, placed too close to the edge of the sideboard, creep to the edge and plunge to pieces with each tremor.

"Both of you," Abby cried. "Stay where you are!" To me, she merely said, "Earthquake."

More rattling, shouting and crashes filled the air— both inside the house and beyond. Something heavy and metal moaned, as if a boat were running aground. Stella appeared in the doorway of the kitchen, a cut on her forehead.

"You all right, ma'am?" she asked.

"Stella!" Mrs. Granville exclaimed. "You're bleeding." She took a step but stumbled, steadying herself on the table.

"Stay put," I told her.

Then I ran to Stella, nodding. "We're fine. But you're hurt," I said. When I looked over her shoulder, a horrible sight greeted my eyes. The kitchen, which was built as an addition on to the back of the original home, sagged, the far wall torn, some of its outer bricks on the kitchen floor, as if the entire room had sheared off into the back alley.

"Come with me," I said, leading her into the steadier part of the house. Steadier—the shaking was stopping. I had her sit down and grabbed a napkin from a sideboard drawer, placing it against the gushing cut on her head. After seeing I had Stella in hand, Mrs. Granville looked around, gathering her wits.

"I need to change, get help." Before I could protest, she rushed from the room, promising to be right back, Abby fast on her heels, urging caution.

I sat with the housekeeper quietly, as if caught in a bubble of time, both of us too shocked to do anything but stare at each other. At last, I seemed to return to my normal senses.

"Let me see what's keeping them," I told Stella, hurrying into the foyer, calling Abby's name. "Is your mother all right?" I asked, heading toward the steps. They seemed to be taking too long. Halfway up, I noticed the stairs had separated from the wall and felt none too secure as I forged upward.

"Abby?" I called again, fearful. Was her mother injured? Where had she gone?

Just as I reached the top, relief flooded me when I saw her coming from her mother's room, her arm around the woman, who'd managed a hurried change of clothes.

"She fell while changing," Abby explained, "but doesn't appear to have broken anything."

Outside, we heard bells clanging, signaling fire patrols and police.

"Let's get her some water," I suggested.

"Or tea would be good," Abby said, leading her mother downstairs. I rushed ahead of them.

Tea—would we be able to heat any water in the kitchen?

When the housekeeper saw me heading to the kitchen, she rose, but I waved her to sit down again, relieved that her head was no longer bleeding. I tiptoed to the woodstove on a few feet of floor not cut off to the ground below, thanking God that the Granvilles had not yet hooked up their kitchen to the city gas lines, and pulled a kettle off a burner. It was hot! I'd be able to make tea.

After accomplishing this task, I brought a teapot and cups on a tray into the dining room.

"I think we should not be using the kitchen for a while," I said to the housekeeper. I poured her a cup of tea, my hand trembling now for real as the minutes' events replayed in my head. An earthquake. What did it do? How many were hurt? Was Ted—

Abby came in and settled her mother in a chair.

"Stella," Mrs. Granville said, alert now, "don't stay. If you'd like to go see to your family, I will not object. I'll assume you'll return when you are satisfied as to their safety. Don't worry about us."

"Thank you so much, Mrs. Granville," Stella said, rising. "I've been thinking of them." Leaving her tea untouched, she hurried toward the kitchen, but I warned her about going in too far. She was able to grab a shawl and bag without venturing beyond the threshold.

But when she opened the front door to make her exit there, we all heard her gasp. We rushed to see what was the matter and were stunned. The path to the door was blocked by several large cornices that had fallen from the rooftop. In addition, bricks lay everywhere, creating a difficult passage.

I raced to the housekeeper's aid, holding her elbow as she stepped up and over obstacle after obstacle, a mountain climber in a city street. She thanked me profusely once we'd reached more level ground, and I returned to the house, only to find Mrs. Granville missing again.

"She's gone to gather her things," Abby said, looking up at the precarious stairway with a worried frown. "I can't seem to stop her! And then she wants to go to the church to see if there's anything to be done to help others."

I looked upstairs and around us. The foyer was relatively unscathed. A mirror hung askew, but other than a few cracks in the plaster and the delicate-looking staircase, it was all right.

"I want to find Ted." I couldn't stop thinking of him. The destruction outside was more than I thought possible. Had he been hurt? I had to tell him…to assure him…I returned his affection. I had to ask him to forgive me for doubting him.

"I'm sure he's—"

An explosion in the distance drowned her last words, making a mockery of her attempt to console. It was so loud and strong that a window beside the door cracked. Another quake?

Abby opened the door and looked around, pointing to smoke blocks away. "Probably a gas line." Another explosion followed, and soon we heard the clanging bells of the fire patrols.

"What was that?" Mrs. Granville said, coming down the stairs as she drew on her gloves.

"Mother, I'm not sure it's a good idea to be out and about," Abby told her, without answering her question.

"What are we supposed to do—wait here for help?"

"I should get to the newspaper," Abby fretted, turning back toward the open door and gazing down the street.

"So, you want me to stay here while you go off?" Mrs. Granville asked.

"I have a job, Mother."

"You think my work is any less worthy just because I do it for free?"

Despite my nerves, I smiled. They were back to their bickering again. In a small way, it felt as if the world had righted itself.

"The church can do without you. The newspaper is probably desperate for reporters…"

"Aha! You think this is your chance. I can understand your eagerness to prove yourself, Abigail, but there might be injured people, people without homes, who need the help of charitable individuals such as myself. And the church is just a few blocks away. I'm sure no harm will befall me on my way."

At the word "befall," the chandelier in the dining room broke free of its ceiling medallion and crashed to the table in a splintering tinkle of glass. We'd just been sitting there a few moments ago!

Mrs. Granville's gloved hand went to her mouth, as Abby hurried to view the destruction. For a moment, we all stared in silent shock.

"I think none of us can say for sure what will *befall* us, Mother," Abby said at last, hands on her hips.

Her eyes wide, Mrs. Granville let out a short, hysterical giggle, a reaction to the tension we were all feeling, and we all laughed, perhaps a little too much because of our nerves. By the time we were done, tears were streaming down our faces. But the laughing fit had the curious effect of calming us, and now we faced reality with open eyes.

"At the church, there will be others to look after your mother," I suggested to Abby, "while she is helping them.

I want to go find Ted, and you can go to the newspaper without worrying about either of us."

"Ted? How on earth will you get to him?" Mrs. Granville asked.

"I'll take one of the horses. I ride quite well, even over obstacles."

"All right," Abby said with determination, clearly not willing to brook objections. "We'll walk Mother to the church. We'll return here and fetch a horse. I don't ride well, so I'll have to piggyback with you, I'm afraid. You can leave me at the newspaper office before going to Ted's boardinghouse."

With that plan settled, we rushed into action.

IT TOOK US nearly two hours to reach the church, a walk that normally only consumed twenty minutes at a leisurely pace.

It was a stroll through a foreign country, ravaged by war. But this war had been wrought by the earth itself, rising up in rebellion against the fragile inhabitants of the city. I murmured many silent prayers on this journey as we encountered other residents suffering from the quake's aftereffects.

A storekeeper begged us to help his wife, trapped in a store room when the door frame collapsed on one side. We worked with a half dozen others to pry the door loose and not a moment too soon—a fire had crept up the block and was fast engulfing nearby buildings.

Many people still wore their nightclothes and wandered streets aimlessly, as if searching for ground not affected by the quake. A mother pushed an empty baby cart with unblinking eyes. A small child sucked his thumb and cried out for his mother. When we couldn't determine his name, only that he'd crawled out of a "hole" when his house fell down, Mrs. Granville took him by the hand to go to the church with her.

A policeman told us that Chinatown was on fire and to stay away. Another directed refugees to a public park.

As we walked, we saw home after home destroyed, often leaning precariously against each other like blocks carelessly stacked. Smoke tinged the air already. More than once we looked at each other as if to say, "How blessed we were that our home didn't collapse." Cracks as wide as craters scarred some streets, and we had to pick our way around rubble while always keeping an eye peeled for falling debris.

By the time we made it to the church, every muscle in my body ached from tensing during the walk. A ride on a horse would be equally harrowing, but I convinced myself I was up to the task.

After Abby made sure her mother was in safe hands with other workers already in aprons handing out tea and bread, we left to return to the house.

"Ruth, I'm not sure it's a good idea for you to search for Ted," Abby confided halfway home. "This is worse than I thought. Maybe we should stay together."

I looked at her, surprised. Did she want my company for her own comfort or for my safety? "I won't rest until I know he's all right." A powerful urge had settled on me, and I wouldn't find peace until I found Ted. I'd misjudged him, and now a cracked and damaged world separated us. A natural disaster—just like the mud slide that had taken my beloved Miguel! The realization was like a horse's kick to my gut. I held my breath for a moment while panic shuddered through me. Ted couldn't be....no, not like Miguel. God surely wouldn't...

"I know he's fine," Abby assured me. "He's strong and resourceful. I suspect he's probably helping others as we speak."

"I have to know," I murmured. Miguel... Ted...perhaps I was too ungrateful...too unaware of my blessings. Was I being punished? I blinked back unshed tears.

Abby put her hand on my arm. "I don't feel right letting you go there. Things are getting worse by the minute. Who knows what you'll encounter? I feel a responsibility for you!"

"I'm sorry, Abby. I simply have to know. I promise you I'll be careful. I will get word to you somehow once I find him. You take care of your mother and your job."

"Ruth, no!" she said, but I quickly put my fingers to her lips before she could say more. It was clear that I couldn't continue walking back to the house with her, or she'd argue the whole way there, trying to wear me down. And by now, it was clear to me that the two of us on a horse's back together would pose more peril than necessary. No, it would be quicker to simply walk to Ted's boardinghouse. I had to see him. I had to apologize. I had to make sure he was all right. *Please, God, let him be all right.*

I grabbed her hands in mine and looked into her eyes. "I swear to you, Abigail Granville, that I will not take undo risks. I swear to you I'll get word back to you and that we'll meet again, if not on this day, then the next. But you cannot stop me from this mission. I have to see Ted and tell him I'm sorry for misjudging him. I'll explain it later."

She let out a frustrated sigh, but then her bright eyes lit up and her dimples deepened. She leaned into me and hugged me close. When she spoke, her voice quavered.

"You be careful, Ruth Sanchez, or my mother will never forgive me for letting you out of my sight."

"You be careful, too, Abby." I was about to thank her for all she'd done for me as a wonderful hostess and new friend, but I refrained from offering those comments, which might have sounded as if I was bidding a more permanent farewell.

With one last hug, we parted.

Chapter Seventeen

OUR PARTING WAS none too soon. Within a few minutes' time, just as I'd managed to make my way around twisted rubble and crumbling sidewalks, the earth shook again. If Abby had been with me, she never would have let me go off on my own.

As it was, I was unable to stay upright. Feeling as if I were a circus performer on a high wire, I reached my arms out for balance to no avail as the ground seemed to rumble and sway. Having experienced the first shock, this one didn't unsettle my soul as much as bring a blanket of discouragement over me. How many more would follow? Would I find Ted alive?

Everywhere I looked there was destruction. The smoke seemed to be building in the east, the air was sharp with the tang of ashes, the buildings around me looked fragile and ready to fall on passers-by. Some of them continued to lose pieces, bricks or roofing, decorative molding, heavy cornices. One had to be looking up constantly at the sound of cracks and crumbling.

The Granvilles lived not far from Washington Street, a road, which I'd learned, stretched in one way or another, not always continuously, from east to west in the city. As I rounded the corner, making my way toward Ted's boardinghouse, I saw that Washington was buckled and cracked, as if a subterranean monster had burrowed its way under the road.

A young woman stood crying outside a home whose top floor had pancaked onto the ground one, the roof now setting atop the windows of the first floor at a dangerously steep angle. Dressed in a nightshirt, her arms bloodied and her face covered with soot and scratches, she wailed, "Papa! Papa!" Just as she seemed about to run back through the open front door, I grabbed and held her.

"No, it's too dangerous, Miss. You can't go in there."

Her frantic eyes turned to me. "No. I heard him cry out. I should have tried harder—"

Just then, a horrible sound rent the air, a screeching and clattering as the roof tiles slid to the ground, and the house shifted once more, its first floor windows crumbling. Entrances were now completely blocked. She sobbed into my shoulder, her fists on my chest.

"There, there," I soothed, my heart breaking for her, and my fear about Ted rising. "Let's get you somewhere safe. We'll let the authorities know your address. They can come back and help dig out the house." I knew her papa was probably lost along with her home, but my gentle prodding gave her the stamina to continue down the street with me, as I searched for a suitable shelter for her.

All the time I walked—stumbled, really—I murmured silent prayers for Ted. *Please let him be all right. Please let him be alive. Please let him be safe.* My stomach roiled at my terrible selfishness, how I'd judged him. And now, would there be an opportunity to set things right? Would I be able to ask for his forgiveness— did I even deserve it?

Many street signs were fallen and under debris, so for a stranger to the city, such as myself, navigation became difficult. "Excuse me, sir, madam," I said over and over again, attempting to find a safe haven for my refugees. Yes, I'd picked up more as I wandered—a young boy and his sister, looking for their parents, an elderly woman who could barely walk, and a Chinaman, whose English was only good enough to talk about a "laundry fire" in animated tones. He'd hoped I'd alert the fire department, I suppose.

But as the smell of smoke grew, I knew in my heart no fire department would be able to fight the blazes. There were too many sources of ignition. As we passed one deep chasm in the road, a flame burst into the air from a broken gas pipe below, causing us to scurry faster, two of us helping the elderly woman rush past the peril.

"Get along, get along," a policeman yelled from atop a horse. "The east side's burning."

The Chinaman looked at me, his eyes wide.

"Sir, do you know…this man's home, he needs help…" My arms ached from helping the old woman, and I felt useless to try to translate the needs of a man whose language I didn't understand. I nudged the Chinaman forward.

Before he could even speak, the policeman shook his head. "Chinatown's gone. Keep moving. We can't help people who don't know enough to get out of harm's way." And with that, he moved on through the growing, moving crowd, issuing his dire warnings.

The Chinaman looked at me, and all I could do was shrug and sigh, gesturing for him to keep walking.

But walk where? At this point, my fears for Ted were compounded by ones for the Granvilles. We shouldn't have separated. Why on earth had we thought that was the best course of action? I was wandering without guidance, and they surely weren't doing any better in this maelstrom.

Dust and smoke clogged the air, and even though the shaking had stopped, walking any street was perilous as damaged buildings continued their descent, chimneys toppling with a rain of dangerous bricks, glass showering from broken windows, beams landing with killing thuds on innocent passers-by.

At the top of a hill, I looked around and saw, down below, smoke billowing as if someone were feeding a gigantic furnace, sending huge clouds of smoke and ash into the air. "Oh, dear, oh dear," I heard someone say, and realized it was my own voice! How lost I felt!

My stragglers stood around me, looking at me as if I knew what to do. I was a stranger here. I wasn't strong or capable of leading them to safety. Why had they chosen me to stay with? Where was Ted, Abby, Mrs. Granville?

I had to choke back my own self-pitying sob then, as I looked around, feeling helpless and lost. I took a deep breath. It wouldn't help anyone if I appeared frightened. I had to keep going—but where?

The Granvilles' church. I knew it was but a few blocks from their house. I remembered walking there with Abby and Mrs. Granville. But it was back from whence we'd come—and smoke was coming from that region, as well.

I saw a man in a cart coming down the road. It was crammed with belongings, with hardly any room, but I boldly strode toward it, holding my hand up to quiet the horse and stop it.

"You'll take these poor folks to safety, sir," I said in a firm voice. I didn't ask. I ordered.

"But—"

Before he could say more, I started helping the older woman onto the bench beside the driver, and I urged the others to clamor on the back.

"You won't get far before more people hop aboard," I said to him. "These are good folks who won't do you any harm. Now, help them, and be grateful they're your passengers and not scalawags!"

His mouth opened, but he said nothing at first. Then, with a sad nod, he said, "What about you, ma'am?"

"I have friends to find. Be on your way…and, thank you."

He flicked the reins and started off, moving toward a part of the city in the west that didn't yet seem touched by fire.

Gathering up my skirts, I turned and walked back toward Washington Street, determined to find the Granvilles' church and Ted.

It took all my willpower, that walk. I had to place a handkerchief over my mouth in order not to choke, and I, like everyone else, had to keep an ear and eye out for falling debris. As I neared the corner of what looked like Washington and California, I saw troops in uniform coming up the street. A commander of some sort was shouting: "This area is cordoned off. Go back!"

No, I couldn't go back! I had to find my friends. I had to find Ted. Surely they were looking for me. Tears stung my eyes, but I was uncertain whether they were from smoke or my own painful longing.

The smoke became my friend, as I was able to hide in it from the soldiers issuing orders—*looters would be shot!*—and scour my memory for where the Granville church might be.

How much time had passed? I had no way of knowing. All markers were gone. No church bells tolled the hour, and the sun's position was obscured by smoke. I felt as if I'd been wandering for days, not hours, and I wondered if this was what it felt like to be completely cut off from God's grace—a terrible thought. After what seemed ages, I'd gone only a few blocks, when at last, I heard a voice, Ted's voice!

Was I imagining it? Was I hallucinating? No, it was him, calling me. "Ruth! Ruth! Over here!"

No, it had to be a dream. It couldn't be him. Fatigue weighted me to the ground, making my feet feel like lead blocks. My head ached—I'd received a glancing blow from a falling brick earlier in my wanderings—and the difficulty in breathing had made my head light and dizzy.

I whirled around, searching this way, that way. *Ted, Ted? Oh, please, Lord, let it be Ted.*

Finally, as a strong wind blew up Washington Street, the clouds cleared, and I saw him! He stood only fifty yards away, helping some people—was it Abby, Mrs. Granville?—onto a cart!

"Ted!" I cried, weeping for joy. "Ted!" I started to run and saw his face turn to me. As he began to come my way, he stopped and shouted, "No, wait!" pointing upward.

It was too late. Before I could decipher his meaning, a roar of bricks and screeching wood surrounded me, and the world went dark.

Chapter Eighteen

WARMTH AND LOVE blanket me. All is pitch-black, and the acrid smell of something burning fills the air.

Do not be afraid, a voice whispers to me in Spanish.

Miguel?

My heart races. *Miguel, how did you find me?* Joy suffuses my being. He wasn't dead?

Miguel, I say, a little irritated now. *How could you let me think you were gone? How cruel that was! It was no joke to me!*

Listen, Ruth. You must live.

Miguel? My voice quivers. *Where are you, darling? Come back to me....*

He loves you, little one, Miguel says. *And you love him. You are the sister of my heart. Go back to your true Corazon. Live, Ruth, live!*

VOICES. SHOUTING. Far away. Oh, my head throbbed. And my arms—they were pinned under me. I couldn't move. Smoke and dust clogged my lungs. I coughed. I heard flames crackle nearby. No!

"I hear her! She's alive. Help me! Take that shovel—be careful, be careful! Pull the bricks off—take the end of that beam! I see her skirt. Abby, lift that corner. Here, help me with this piece." Ted's voice, strong and firm but filled with a tinge of fear.

"Get moving, you can't stay here," I heard an authoritarian voice say.

"No, our friend is under here—a building collapsed. We saw her—" Abby's voice, followed by Mrs. Granville's, saying, "She is my charge. I cannot leave her."

"You have to leave her. I'm sorry, Miss, but she's probably gone. And the fire's just two houses down. Nobody's going to survive if you don't get out now!"

"No!" Ted roared. "You'll have to shoot me first!" And I heard him scrambling, throwing bricks. "Get over there. Get back to digging. Fast!"

I don't know how long they dug. I drifted back into unconsciousness, and the next thing I remembered was hands under my legs, around my back, Ted's strong arms cradling me.

"Thank the Lord, thank the Lord," Mrs. Granville cried, her voice broken by coughing.

"Let's go," Abby said.

My eyes fluttered open, but as soon as they did, I wished the scene away. Smoke surrounded us, so much so that I had no idea where we were. It was warm— flashes of orange to our backs and sides indicated we were inside the inferno. Oh, no, had they lingered too long? They should have left and saved themselves.

I tried to whisper these thoughts, but Ted shushed me. "Rest, Ruth."

"Over here!" he cried. "I know there's a path this way."

For what seemed like hours, he carried me. I knew it tired him—I could hear him breathing fast, could feel his heart beating at a gallop's pace near my ear, nestled into his chest. I tried to protest, to say I could walk, but he would hear none of it, and I stopped trying to convince him when I realized he was using precious energy arguing against me.

By now, we'd started hearing explosions, and I heard Abby explain to her mother that the soldiers had told her they were dynamiting sections of town to set up "fire breaks."

Onward our party went. Ted didn't stop walking, even when it was clear he'd reached a dead-end at one point. He just turned around and marched out, choosing another route. The Granvilles were uncharacteristically silent, a testament to our dire circumstances—Abby's opinions were muted.

Finally, after several switchbacks and false turns, I sniffed and smelled something in the air—saltwater. Ted was finding the way.

Within a few blocks, the smoke lessened considerably, and we joined a parade of refugees headed for encampments that seemed to be springing up in public parks.

"Do you need help, sir?" A dark-suited man with bushy moustache and his sleeves rolled up came up to us. "I'm a doctor. I have set up a tent for the hurt."

They carried me to that tent, where Ted laid down his burden, at last. He refused to leave at first, but the doctor wouldn't examine me in front of a man, so Abby stepped in, assuring Ted she'd look after me.

"Get some water," Abby told him softly. "Mother needs some, and I'm sure you could use a drink."

A quick examination revealed I'd been spared great harm. Other than a bump on my head and superficial scrapes and bruising, I was unscathed. No broken bones or punctured lungs. No grievous injuries. Still feeling winded but recovering my strength, I insisted on leaving the tent so that the good doctor and volunteer nurses could help others, worse off than I was.

The city continued to be rocked by explosions, as more dynamite was laid and ignited. But still smoke poured from its western fringes. The Granville home was surely lost.

As I stood looking into the distance, thinking of all the people lost in the destruction, Ted came up behind me, placing his hand gently in mine.

I turned to look at him. "Ted, I don't know how to begin to thank you. I heard you—you insisted on staying to dig me out."

He sucked in his lower lip, opened his mouth to speak but closed his eyes and looked away. Then, his eyes open and staring at me as if looking into my heart, he said, "In that moment, I was more afraid than I'd ever been, that I'd lost you…" He pulled me to him in a shuddering hug, his breath in my hair. "Ruth, I thought you were gone from me forever."

Despite my best efforts, I started to weep. I'd felt the same way looking for him, I realized, and only now that we were safe did I allow myself to give voice to those fears. I told him I'd felt he'd been taken from me, I blubbered about how sorry I was for my behavior the night before, I said I was selfish and judgmental, but he would have none of it.

Pulling apart, he placed his finger on my lips. His eyes glistening, he said, "No more of that. We should thank God for our safety and help those not as fortunate."

So, standing in a circle with Abby and Mrs. Granville, we held hands and prayed our gratitude, beseeching God to give comfort and succor to those who were in need.

Once that prayer was over, though, it was clear Mrs. Granville and Abby had no intention of waiting for the Lord to provide.

"I want to help the doctors," Mrs. Granville said. "I can do a little nursing."

"Mother, you're weak. Rest a while. I'll go offer our help."

"Nonsense, Abby! I'm fine. You're a bit squeamish about medical things. You're likely to create problems rather than solve them should you faint at the slightest pinprick..."

"Mother, I've been helping people all morning..."

Ted and I looked at each and smiled. The earth had shaken, yes, but Abby and her mother's relationship was without cracks or disruptions.

DESPITE OUR DESIRE to help, we were all ailing and unable to do as much as we would have liked. Mrs. Granville had to take frequent breaks to catch her breath—the smoke seemed to have damaged her lungs. And I, too, felt the need for rest often. Usually, it was Ted or Abby who sensed these times and insisted I sit down or drink or eat something. They must have made a secret pact to make sure I wouldn't overdo.

Safe from the fires, we set about helping the injured, binding wounds and bringing supplies to the doctors and nurses in the park. Ted also helped unload some food supplies from several wagons, items donated by local restaurants, some of which were too damaged to do business anyway.

Abby gathered information while she worked, playing reportress without a printed sheet to carry her words. She would pass along news—real news, not rumors—only after verifying facts as best she could, usually finding sources who were at the places the situations occurred. During the course of the afternoon and evening, she was able to tell us:

"All the plate glass windows are out of buildings on Grant Street, the chimney stack on the power house, the steeple of St. Patrick's. The Strathmore Hotel's walls are gone….The Valencia Street Hotel—it's as if a giant picked up its upper floor and flung it onto the street. People are moving things out of Central Hospital. A Brigadier General Funston volunteered to help—he's the one who got the soldiers to our neighborhood so quickly, by sending messages to Fort Mason and the Presidio! The destruction is terrible, the stories—oh, the stories are too awful to bear, people trapped as the flames engulf dwellings—I could barely take them down through my own tears….a herd of cattle ran free up Mission Street!"

She wrote them all down in her small notebook, and I knew one day she'd tell the tale in full.

All over the park, tents were going up, and somehow Ted managed to secure two for us, made of old sheets and blankets. Our clothing was soiled beyond relief, but we managed to scrub out the worst of it and carry on.

THE NEXT DAY, the destruction became even clearer as more and more poured into our encampment. We learned of other such camps, some even with names – Harbor View and Lobos Square, for example.

Food might not have been plentiful, but it was sufficient, and we soon learned that the entire country was rushing to our aid, with a hospital train headed west from Virginia and every single tent in the U.S. military's possession either in the city or on its way. This, too,

Abby told us, was the result of this General Funston, who'd petitioned the Secretary of War, William Howard Taft, for the supplies. Hundreds of thousands of rations came our way from the Vancouver Barracks on the Canadian Border.

It was both wonderful and horrible to contemplate— the collapse of the city and yet the breadth of support from so many strangers.

I worried about my family worrying, but that fear was soon relieved when the post office opened two days after the quake, promising citizens that for the price of a two-cent stamp, telegrams would be delivered within the city. Outgoing mail was as scrupulously handled, and I penned a fast note assuring my parents that we were all well and that I would come home as soon as I possibly could, but they shouldn't worry in the meantime.

Rain came at last on the third day, and finally, finally, the fires were extinguished.

But Mrs. Granville's cough was no better. If anything, it seemed worse, perhaps because of the dampness that now surrounded us. As she rested one evening, I pulled Ted and Abby aside around a campfire.

"I would like to offer you all the hospitality of my home," I said softly. "If we can find someone to take us to a rail line south of here, it won't be long before we are in Monterey. We can telegraph my family from the train station."

"I have to reach my grandfather," Ted protested. He'd already sent a letter to San Quentin, requesting more time due to the earthquake. I doubted they'd deny the request.

"You can't reach him from here, Ted," Abby said, reflecting on my proposal. "But you might be able to cable him from somewhere else."

She looked at me. "Mother will want to stay and help," she said, anguish in her voice. Clearly she didn't favor that plan.

"You'll have to help convince her to leave, Abby. I think she needs fresh air and rest," I said, with Ted nodding agreement.

"Maybe if I tell her I'll stay and continue working…" Abby began, but both Ted and I were shaking our heads before she could finish.

"No," I said, reaching for her hand. "She'll only leave if you do. Try to convince her—she might be tempted by the chance to see my parents and grandparents. We'll use that."

Abby ultimately agreed, and we decided to present our plan to her the next morning and try to find transportation out of the city as soon as possible.

IN THE MORNING, however, Mrs. Granville seemed more determined than ever to stay in San Francisco. Even the lure of seeing my family wasn't sufficient to pry her away. She only promised to "catch up with us," after she felt the city was returning to normal.

Ted, Abby and I joined forces, though, and when Ted was able to secure us a place on a wagon heading south the following day, we insisted she accompany us. Abby threatened to join the suffragette movement if she didn't—and later confided to me, after her mother's capitulation, that she would probably join it anyway.

We couldn't stop Mrs. Granville from continuing to help our last day in camp, though. She worked tirelessly that afternoon, only leaving the medical tents when doctors and nurses forced her out.

I understood why it was so hard to pull herself away. Despite all the death and injury, people were found alive, were recovering from their blows. It was an affirmation of God's love to see life springing afresh from all these ashes.

Late that evening, before we were going to break for our meal, a man was brought into the medical tent on a stretcher. He'd been found amidst a pile of rubble near downtown, the only survivor of a bank building that had fallen. Rescuers only located him, they said, when a dog wouldn't stop barking near where he was buried.

His bright blue eyes flickered as they brought him into the tent, and it was clear he was injured grievously. Blood trickled from the corner of his mouth, and his breathing was more like panting, accompanied by a soft whistling wheeze.

"Here, get him some water," Mrs. Granville instructed, and I quickly found a tin cup into which I poured some clear liquid.

He sipped it thirstily, but pushed us away after he was finished.

"Help others," he managed to whisper as a nurse came by to check him.

"We'll do that, as soon as we get you settled," Abby chided. "Don't make a fuss now."

"Here, let me at least wipe you off to see how you are injured," Mrs. Granville said, coming forward with a pail of soapy water into which she dipped a cloth. As Abby and I held him in a sitting position, she began her ministrations.

She started with his dusty face, tenderly cleaning it of soot and ash, while Abby gently asked me to fetch more water. It was clear he was parched. "See if there's some soft bread, too," she called after me, "and some milk."

"Sir," Mrs. Granville asked as I walked away. "Might we trouble you to tell us who you are? Perhaps there is someone we can notify on your behalf."

"John Templeton," he wheezed. Clearly, talking was difficult. "Help others," he repeated.

Soon, I returned with a mug of milk and a plate of buttered bread, handing them over to Abby. "You're probably half starved," she said to the man. "So try to eat something. It will give you your strength back."

The nurse whispered to us that he needed a doctor's attention: "He might have a pierced lung," she said, hurrying away.

Whether from pain or a desire not to take food someone else might need more, Mr. Templeton wouldn't eat the bread, just sadly shaking his head no.

"Come now, there's plenty to go around, Mr. Templeton," Abby scolded. "Don't be foolish."

"Abby, the man is hurt. Don't insult him," Mrs. Granville said to her daughter. She turned back to him. "Here, let me wipe this blood away from around your mouth." He'd sustained a cut on his nose, and the dried blood covered his upper lip, now faint with a fresh moustache.

"A horse, Jezzy, was with me. Is she okay?" he wheezed.

"Jezzy?" I asked. The name was familiar.

"Jezebel," he whispered. "Not mine. Keeping her."

Jezebel. It came to me—Mr. Crane's horse! What had happened to it when he'd gone to prison? My pulse pounded. Could this be...I ran out of the tent with no explanation, searching for Ted. Finding him by our tent gathering belongings, I breathlessly asked him my question. "Your grandfather's horse—who'd he give him to when he was arrested? Do you know?"

Ted scratched his head. "That was before I came west, before the trial. I don't know. He probably just left her where she was, in her stable. Why?"

I didn't answer, just grabbed his hand and pulled him back to the medical tent.

Once inside, we hurried to Mr. Templeton where Mrs. Granville was finished washing the man's face.

And there, in the dim light, was the evidence we needed—the small half-moon scar on the man's upper lip, just as Ted's grandfather had described it. The preacher—Mr. Crane's alibi—we'd found him!

"Mr. Templeton," I said, my voice shaking. "I need you to meet someone." I quickly introduced them, and Ted skillfully asked questions to elicit whether or not Mr. Templeton had met his grandfather in the hills the day the robbery and murder took place. He was very careful not to reveal why he was asking, lest the man's charitable impulses urge him to create a story in order to save a man's life.

Recognizing that the man was tired and hurt, Ted kept his questions simple. But he quickly found out that Mr. Templeton was a stable worker, that he was devout, and, yes, he remembered Ted's grandfather on the day of the robbery. He noted such things in his journal, he said, patting a pocket.

Tears of joy choked me, and Ted was just as visibly moved, his voice quavering as he thanked the man over and over again, as he assured him he would be fine.

Mr. Templeton gave us a wan smile. "I know I will be fine," he said. "Go tend to others."

We did as he said only because we knew it would distress him to have us linger and because the nurse returned at that moment with the doctor, but our hearts were lightened. Ted's grandfather could be cleared now! Ted could save him from the gallows! Something good had come out of all this destruction.

Throughout the next few hours I prayed silently, alternating between songs of thanksgiving and pleas to help us as we attempted to aid others. Mr. Templeton's wasn't the only resurrection that evening. Several other people were brought to our aid station who'd been discovered beneath the rubble. The entire medical group was rejoicing as life after life was saved.

But as twilight approached, the tide turned. Mrs. Granville approached our campfire with two small books in her hands.

"I've bad news. Mr. Templeton passed," she said simply. "But here is his journal and his Bible. I thought you might be able to find the relevant passage about your grandfather in it, Ted."

He nodded grimly, taking the thin leather-bound notebook from her and flipping to the dates in question. "He told the truth," he said after a while with a sad excitement. "He describes my grandfather, mentions him by name, tells of his 'soul's torment'." He looked at me, his eyes glistening. "What a wonderful man he was!"

All I could do was nod in return. Words failed me. "I wonder if he had any family," I murmured.

"We'll do our best to find out," Mrs. Granville said.

"And let them know what good he has done," Ted added. "I can have you and Ruth and Abby swear out affidavits, confirming what he said about Grandfather. And this journal will give weight to your testimony." He flipped through the pages of the journal. "This book catalogs his encounters with other lost souls like my grandfather. He ministered to them all, just an ordinary man living his faith."

Would that we all could be as kind and loving as he had been, I thought.

Ted pointed to the book in my hand. "That's his Bible?"

"Yes," I said, letting it flip open to the page last marked with a ribbon. It was Psalm 75:

> *Unto thee, O God, do we give thanks, unto thee do we give thanks: for that thy name is near thy wondrous works declare.*
> *When I shall receive the congregation I will judge uprightly.*
> *The earth and all the inhabitants thereof are dissolved: I bear up the pillars of it. Selah.*
> *I said unto the fools, Deal not foolishly: and to the wicked, Lift not up the horn:*
> *Lift not up your horn on high: speak not with a stiff neck.*
> *For promotion cometh neither from the east, nor from the west, nor from the south.*
> *But God is the judge: he putteth down one, and setteth up another.*
> *For in the hand of the LORD there is a cup, and the wine is red; it is full of mixture; and he poureth out of the same: but the dregs thereof, all the wicked of the earth shall wring them out, and drink them.*
> *But I will declare for ever; I will sing praises to the God of Jacob.*
> *All the horns of the wicked also will I cut off; but the horns of the righteous shall be exalted.*

"The earth...is dissolved," I murmured. My face turned toward Ted's. "He must have been reading this as comfort."

Mrs. Granville took the Bible from me. "You keep the journal, Ted, but I'll place this somewhere safe. If we locate his family, we should give it to them."

We went back to our arduous labor, but thrumming in the back of my mind was this line from the psalm: *But God is the judge...*

God was the judge, not me. I'd judged Ted unfairly, linking his character to that of his grandfather's before Mr. Crane had changed. How easy it had been to do! Although he'd forgiven me, even graciously pointing out how he could have allayed my fears by a simple confession of his father's story, I still felt I had to make it up to him in some way.

Chapter Nineteen

THE NEXT MORNING, despite Mrs. Granville's protests that she wanted to continue helping, we bundled her into the wagon Ted had managed to find headed south to the first available stop on the rail line. From there, we'd buy tickets using money Ted would withdraw from the bank.

Ted was frantic to reach his grandfather—to let prison authorities and the court know he'd found the alibi witness. He wouldn't leave San Francisco without first sending another letter—who knew when it would reach the prison? And then, once we reached my family, he immediately telegraphed San Quentin from the station in Watsonville, where we disembarked.

My parents, so relieved to have us all safe, welcomed him with loving, open arms. Many tears of joy flowed as we embraced, and I was unashamed to tell my mother how much I'd missed her and how glad I was to see her again. She dissolved into hiccupping sobs in my arms, so happy was she to hear those words.

How good it felt to sink into a foamy bath that night, washing the grime of the earthquake from my body and putting on clean clothes at last. Abby was outfitted with something from my store of clothes, with her mother commenting how nice it was to see her daughter in a well-laundered outfit for a change. Mrs. Granville was dressed with care by my mother, who was overjoyed to see her older friend from childhood days.

As for Ted, Josephus and Father found sufficient clothing for him, and it delighted me how natural he looked in ranch things, instead of the suits he'd worn in the city.

Anita and her family had gone on their way by now, but she'd left a loving note for me, telling me that she hoped I would still think of her as a sister, regardless of Miguel's passing. I wrote her back immediately, promising to continue our friendship.

The second night in the valley, I gave my parents Mr. Crane's apology, which was crinkled and smudged from its time in the pocket of my dress on the day of the earthquake, and they read it in sad silence. But they listened to my tale of meeting him face-to-face, my mother asking some pointed questions to satisfy her mind and heart. Ted had offered to be part of this meeting, but I'd told him it would be easier on my parents to be able to speak freely without worry of offending him.

In the end, mother agreed to share the note with my grandparents, and I saw her doing so on the back veranda the next evening. In the middle of this scene, Ted appeared out back. I was about to go fetch him so he wouldn't interfere in my grandmother's reading of the apology, but I stopped myself when I saw her wipe a tear from her eye and immediately embrace Ted.

"It was good of you to bring this," I heard her say. "It is a blessing to read."

The next few days were filled with blessings, in fact. The Granvilles stayed with my grandparents while Ted bunked with Josephus, and we had several merry dinners together, despite the shadows that haunted us all.

Whether it was the fresh air, sunshine or good company, Mrs. Granville's health improved quickly.

Josephus did his best to hide his disappointment in Sally's engagement, which he knew about by now, but I saw him drift into silent brooding more than a few times.

And, of course, the Granvilles were eager for news of San Francisco and how friends and acquaintances had fared. They read reports whenever they could get their hands on one. Abigail was fit to be tied, restless to head back north to continue reporting. She wrote a first-person account of the quake for our local newspaper and received many accolades for her fine writing and reporting. This soothed her, but she still chomped at the bit. The only thing keeping her tethered to us was her concern for her mother. But as Mrs. Granville's health improved dramatically, the two recommenced their sparring. It was a relief to hear it return.

As for Ted…he spent part of each day working on briefs and communications to file with the court after receiving word that his grandfather's execution would, in fact, be delayed. This was due to the earthquake as much as to Ted's work. Many people associated with the court couldn't be mustered to hear a case.

A week into his stay, however, a rider came to the ranch with a telegraph that changed everything.

I knew he was hoping this would be an announcement of his day in court on behalf of his grandfather at last, so I was quick to take notice.

I'd been sitting in the parlor trying to intercede in a discussion between Abby and her mother about when they would return home—Abby was arguing for a speedy trip and Mrs. Granville was trying to convince her to wait just another week so she could visit longer with my parents and grandparents. Poor Mrs. Granville—although she'd planned on selling her house, she now admitted to feeling sorrow that it was lost and struggling to accept that all her mementoes were also gone. "It was part of my husband's family's legacy," she said with a mournful smile. "And I must confess to having not realized how much I liked that connection to Alfred. I dare say I'd have had trouble letting it go." At this, Abby agreed, consoling her mother that they'd have to build new memories together. It was their usual loving banter—I'd had to explain to my mother how this was their regular form of communication the second night they were here.

They were in a thicket of words when I heard the horseman come and saw my mother go to greet him. When she received the telegram, she immediately called out for Ted, who'd been helping Josephus repair a nearby bench.

He ripped open the telegram alone on the front veranda—my mother and brother had had the wisdom to retreat, leaving him to receive his news in private—and I saw his shoulders sag as he read the missive.

Knowing Abby and her mother wouldn't miss me, I rushed outside, touching Ted lightly on the arm as he stared down at the paper.

"What is it? Don't tell me they're denying your request for a new hearing!"

He shook his head. "It won't be necessary now," he said softly. "Grandfather is dead. Died in his sleep."

"Oh, Ted." I reached up to embrace him, and he folded me in his strong arms, smelling of the sun and the ranch. I felt his shuddering sigh and knew how this grieved him. "You did everything you could. You would have cleared him!"

"The doctor should have seen him," he said through gritted teeth. "And I wasn't there to comfort him. I don't even know if he had been given news of the new evidence. He might have died thinking he was never going to be proven innocent."

I closed my eyes, remembering my conversation with Mr. Crane.

"There's a peace in it," he'd told me of his incarceration. "Knowing you're paying somehow for all you done wrong. Hard as it is, there's a peace in it. But I don't want to burden nobody now. And I know if it should come out I was not guilty, some poor fellow here will have it on his soul that he led an innocent man to the noose. That doesn't sit lightly with me, Miss Ruth."

What Ted didn't know was that his grandfather would never have felt "innocent," that he'd gracefully accepted his imprisonment, almost seen it as a gift, a physical way to show the Lord he was sorry. And the only thing that troubled him about it was the possibility that someone would lead him to the gallows and later find out he'd not committed the crime for which he was hanged. He'd avoided that fate and also the better one Ted had envisioned for him—living out his few remaining years free and clear. Except he would have never felt "cleared."

These thoughts I kept to myself, knowing they'd offer little comfort when the cut was so raw.

"I'll have to see to a burial," he said. "I'll wire about that. I—I need to go into town. I—" Rattled by the news, he seemed adrift.

"I'll get my brother, and we'll both go with you."

"Thank you, Ruth. Thank you. For everything."

I stared at him. "I should thank you. You saved my life. And I treated you poorly. I judged you wrongly, based on nothing but who your grandfather was—or used to be. That was a sinful thing to do, and I'm mightily sorry. Can you forgive me?"

He didn't answer. He just swept the big hat off his head that he'd borrowed from Joe, and bent me back for a pure, sweet kiss.

THE MONTHS THAT followed were filled with life and death. The death, of course, had been Ted's grandfather's, but the business of it took a while to be resolved. It turned out the prison had arranged for a burial in a small cemetery near its walls, overlooking the bay. Ted managed to pull a memorial service together for his grandfather, and my parents granted me permission to attend it with him without a chaperone. By that time, Abby and Mrs. Granville had returned to San Francisco, both of them intent on helping rebuild the city in their own ways. Their house was gone, but they bought the smaller abode Mrs. Granville had claimed to want and set up housekeeping immediately, connecting with a new church and doing what they could to help their neighbors.

And by that time, I was Ted's fiancée—he'd asked my father for my hand the night before receiving the news of his grandfather's passing, and he sprang the question to me the next evening, not caring, he said, if it was unseemly after such news because the earthquake had taught him not to delay happiness.

With great joy, I accepted his loving request, and my mother and I began the pleasant task of planning a wedding for some time that fall. Ted's sister would come from New York, and the Granvilles would repeat their journey south for this glad occasion.

Before heading back north for the memorial service, I took my favorite mare out for a long, dusty ride on an afternoon brilliant with warm sunshine. I rode past two ranches before I came to the little glade I'd been heading for, and pulled some wild roses from my saddle bag, strolling toward a neat enclosure at the end of a pasture. A wrought iron fence surrounded a handful of gravestones. The freshest of these, still pearly white, was Miguel's.

After placing the roses at the grave and murmuring a prayer for the repose of his soul, I sat and stroked the stone, as if it were Miguel's strong shoulder. When I spoke, it was in English and Spanish:

"I hope you are at peace, my dear, and happy for the news I must share. A fine man has asked for my hand, and I've said I will marry him. He knows of you and respected my grief at your passing. But I know you would be angry if I were to stay in widow's weeds my whole life, mourning what was not to be. I love him, Miguel, with my whole heart. And I know you would be happy for me. I will never forget you, dear, but he is my *Corazon* now. And you will forever be a deeply loved brother. I am going to live, my dear, as you told me I should."

Touching my lips with my fingers, I placed this second-hand kiss on the grave, stood and walked back to my horse. Then I rode home to Ted, my once-shattered heart mended at last, lighter and happier than I ever could have imagined two years ago.

If you enjoyed this book, you might also like Libby Sternberg's *Kit Austen's Journey,* the story of Ruth's grandparents.

Acknowledgements

My sincere thanks go to Cara Randall, librarian at the California State Railroad Museum, and her colleagues, especially Kyle Wyatt, curator, who helped find information for me on the ferries crossing the bay to get to San Quentin. Thanks, too, to Nancy Nies, California native and my cousin's wife, for pointing me to that institution.

It was difficult to capture in my characters' points of view the entirety of the devastation wrought on San Francisco during the 1906 earthquake and its aftermath, but two books in particular were extremely helpful: Simon Winchester's *A Crack in the Edge of the World* and Malcolm E. Barker's compilation of first-hand accounts in *Three Fearful Days*. I recommend them to readers who want to read more expansive tales of the earthquake.

As always, I'm grateful to my family for their support of my writing habit, particularly my husband, who was a thoughtful and tactful first editor of Ruth's story. *Libby Sternberg*

ABOUT THE AUTHOR

Libby Sternberg is the author of women's fiction, historical and young adult novels. She received an Edgar nomination for her first young adult mystery and writes humorous women's fiction under the name Libby Malin. All her books have been critically acclaimed. She lives in Pennsylvania with her husband and has three children, of whom she is immensely proud. Visit her website at www.LibbySternberg.com.

About Istoria Books

Istoria Books is a boutique publisher handling only fiction, selecting books we consider to be "good stories, well told."

All our books are very competitively priced, and we run many discount specials.

Visit the Istoria Books website (www.IstoriaBooks.com) and sign up for the mailing list to learn of special discounts and deals.

Literary, Mystery, Romance, Women's Fiction, Short Stories, Historical and more...

Istoria Books
www.IstoriaBooks.com